Virginia Vaughan

The New Era

a Dramatic Poem

Virginia Vaughan

The New Era
a Dramatic Poem

ISBN/EAN: 9783337206628

Printed in Europe, USA, Canada, Australia, Japan

Cover: Foto ©Andreas Hilbeck / pixelio.de

More available books at **www.hansebooks.com**

THE NEW ERA.

THE NEW ERA

A DRAMATIC POEM

BY

VIRGINIA VAUGHAN.

"Con questa filosofia l'anima mi aggrandisce e mi si magnifica l'intelletto."
GIORDANO BRUNO

LONDON:
CHAPMAN & HALL (Limited),
193, PICCADILLY.
1880.

London : Printed by A. Schulze, 13, Poland Street.

Dramatis Personæ.

———

HESPERUS. } *An Italian youth killed in battle during the siege of Rome.*

HYPERION.
PROCYON.
ORION.
AGLAIA.
ISIS.
} *Group of Celestials who have protected Hesperus during his life, and whom he joins on entering the higher sphere in which they dwell after his death.*

UNA . . . *Queen of the Celestial Sphere.*

VITTORIA
FIOMBINI.
} *A Roman Princess placed under the guardianship of Hesperus.*

FEDERICO
PIOMBINI.
} *A Roman Prince, the relation and lover of Vittoria.*

JOSEPH
MAZZINI.
} *Italian patriot and statesman.*

KING OF HARMONIA.

QUEEN OF HARMONIA.

POETS OF THE PLANET MIRA.

CHORUSES OF THE ANGELIC HOSTS.

SPIRITS OF THE SANCTUARY.

DEDICATION.

———◦◦◦———

To R. S.

Large-natured man to every woe inclined,
With open palm outstretched to aid distress
At each appeal, and the world's wrongs redress,
As free in bounty as the summer wind,
Thou, and those like to thee, redeem mankind.
True, gentle, wise, to name thee is to bless ;
The generous years thy reverend brow caress
With memories sweet, thou movest love-entwined.
I sing the song of the great future's gain,
When love's serener law all shall obey,
But if that happy shore we e'er attain,
Souls such as thine will guide us on the way,
Who vanquish in the present grief and pain,
And change our twilight gloom to perfect day.

PREFACE.

This poem was written with the conviction that many of the great philosophical and religious questions which the scientific mind of the present day has condemned as being beyond the sphere of human inquiry, are nevertheless not only true but capable of demonstration, and are destined in time to be verified by science itself; the existence and nature, for example, of the Supreme Spirit of the universe, the fact of a future life, the unity of the human and divine nature, the interdependence and brotherhood of the infinite series of races that law and analogy compel us to believe people the universe, and other kindred doctrines.

Instead of advocating this philosophy directly, from a didactic point of view, I have tried the experiment of giving it a new vitality by showing it in action ; presenting it upon the living and moving stage of a dramatic poem.

The scheme of the celestial spheres discussed in the opening scene of this poem, rests upon a belief in the necessary relation and correspondence of the visible and invisible domains of nature, the responsive realms of one marvellous and mystical whole ; a subtle and exquisite theory which has already received a certain amount of support from philosophical and scientific inquirers, and which here at least is accepted without reserve. The knowledge which we can now claim to possess of the plurality of worlds—the very doctrine, by the way, which Giordano Bruno, whose noble words stand upon my title page, was burnt to death for proclaiming—renders it inevitable almost, if we believe at all in a future life, that we should admit the corresponding fact of a plurality of heavens. This hypothesis is adopted in the accompanying poem, and the sphere which is its theatre of action is presented as the heaven merely of our own planet.

The political doctrine advanced in the second scene is again an application of one of the fundamental principles of the same philosophy, a belief in the nobility, dignity and freedom of human nature; while it carries moreover to its logical conclusion the theory of the organic unity of the race, taught by Auguste Comte and earlier writers. When a race considered as an organism, a collective and universal being, the humanity of modern scientific worship, has attained a high degree of civilization, it is required according to the doctrine here insisted upon, to organize a social condition befitting its power and maturity; an era of peace and order that will prove the fulfilment of the prophecy of early ages; and failing to make this transition, it will be doomed to deterioration and decay; just as the individual who becomes a man must forego the follies of youth and enter upon a noble and honourable career, at the cost of losing his reputation and finding his life branded with the stigma of failure and defeat.

The revolutionary movement of thirty years ago is assumed, not without justification from the facts of history, to have been the first decisive effort of the European nations to initiate this great reform. The effort failed in consequence of the blindness and apathy of the governments, and that failure was marked by the fall of Mazzini in Rome, and the triumph of Louis Napoleon in Paris. We are now reaping in the whirlwind the bitter fruits of the seeds that were then sown upon the wind, and the real problem confronting the statesmen of our own day is to retrieve the defeat of that frustrate revolution, to escape from the epoch of retrogression and violence into which we then entered, and inaugurate even at this late day the era of peace and brother-hood upon which the welfare of the future depends.

This volume, if I carry out my present de-sign, will be a link, partly dramatic and partly philosophic, between two dramas, more strictly speaking, which will treat respectively the early

experiences of Hesperus in the Ethereal Sphere
to which he ascends when killed at the siege of
Rome, and the life of Vittoria Piombini, swayed
and coloured by the opposing influences of her
good and evil genius, Hesperus and Federico.
My aim in these poems will be, I need scarcely
say, to make them depend entirely for their
interest and claim to attention upon their in-
trinsic poetic merit, the force and dramatic
truth with which they are presented ; while at
the same time the scheme proposed will call for
a discussion in them of questions of most deep
and vital significance. The sublime and pathetic
scenes of the initiation of Hesperus in heaven,
should I succeed in doing justice to my own
vision of that great theme, must, as it seems to
me, cast a new light upon the whole subject of
a future life and others of equal importance.
In the present book this lovely youth, in a twofold sense a child in heaven, since he was a
mere youth at the time of his death, and is now
the youngest soul of a race of transcendent
wisdom and experience, appears as an inquirer

into the mysteries that have hitherto baffled him, and enters for the first time into the full activity and enjoyment of his new and beneficent career.

The poem now presented to the public, I was persuaded (self-persuaded), to finish and publish before its predecessor, in the vague expectation that the glowing scenes described upon the planet Mira might perchance bring some message of peace and good-will to our harassed and afflicted governments. An author must be excused for falling in love with his own conceptions while in the act of composition, and I confess that this scene was written with a great elation of spirit, and in the full persuasion that it could not fail to produce an effect in inducing a better order of things upon our own planet. Now that the golden gate of the ideal world has swung back and closed against me, I perceive how unlikely it is that such good fortune should attend any work of the imagination, even although a thousand fold more persuasive and powerful, more sweet and seductive than this too crude and imperfect poem; still I may at least express a hope that some quickening thought in these pages may, through the action of another mind, become a deed or blow in behalf of harmony and the future.

The New Era which, according to my doctrine, ought to be established to-day in Europe, is supposed to have been inaugurated upon the planet Mira a century ago. The Congress there convened meets to proclaim the happiness of the peoples, and to celebrate their great achievements in art, in literature, in science and government, during a period of unexampled progress and prosperity. I will conclude with a devout prayer that our own monarchs and statesmen, the powers that be upon this globe, may emulate the example of the noble Miranites of an earlier generation, and transmit to their descendants the priceless inheritance of a redeemed and regenerated world.

V. V.

Queen Anne's Mansions, St. James' Park.
September, 1880.

THE NEW ERA.

SCENE I.—*Celestial Sphere. Isis and Hesperus are discovered seated and conversing in a pavilion in a beautiful grove, near a magnificent Palace built of a single pearl.*

Hesperus.

In my new life in this ethereal sphere,
Full fraught with rich experiences and joys,
'Tis still the mystery of mine own soul
At which I marvel most ; my boundless scope,
Vast range, and ever new intensity
Of feeling and of thought ; a depth of life
Whereof on earth in ignorance I lived,
My highest raptures there a languid flame,
Too feeble to resound my human lyre,
Or to re-echo in immortal strain,
Celestial harmonies.   In noonday calm,
In this balm breathing fragrant grove reclined,

My ravished gaze fed by these heavenly scenes,
Thou by my side with inmost sympathy
To each unuttered thought flashing response,
Thus only to my consciousness revealed,
Unnoted else their vague and shadowy flight,
In such an hour, the waves that lap my shore,
Low murmuring billows of that viewless sea,
Which clasps with wide embrace the Universe,
Are Infinite.   Faint with excess of bliss,
Like some new kindled sun my spirit glows,
A sun of love, whose pure and ardent rays
Stream unimpeded forth through orb-lit space,
Touching, on their bright path, unnumbered worlds,
Glancing o'er countless souls, and quickening them
With mine own life.   Dream-like before me now
In swift succession palpable they rise,
Those whirling orbs, those fleeting human lives,
And float a glimmering vision on the air,
By my ecstatic mind vaguely discerned.
My being is transmuted all to love.
And by that word, in heaven, on earth supreme,
That sacred spell and that supernal law,
Thee, Isis, I constrain.   This is the hour,
Most sweet, most blest ; thy promise now fulfil,

The subtle mysteries profound of being
As yet ungrasped by my unwonted mind,
Do thou, at last, explain.

Isis.

What wouldst thou, speak?

Hesperus.

The law of life and attributes disclose
Of this transcendent sphere, this radiant realm
Which we name heaven, our home how well-beloved,
Our garb invisible and arm of might,
And wing of flame through vacancy outstretched;
Its nature and its mystery reveal.
How ravishing the scenes which meet my gaze,
These varied landscapes with enchantment veiled,
These vistas of transcendent loveliness,
Fair mounts sunlit, and woods, and flowing streams,
With cities stately fair diversified,
Whose gleaming temples and effulgent shrines
And palaces high reared of flawless gems,
The shimmering splendours of the day reflect;
The bright ideal of some favoured land,
Which might be on the earth; and like the earth,

So sweetest heaven itself with heaven ensphered,
Encradled by the azure infinite,
A dome unfathomable and profound,
Where throbs the sun of this celestial day,
A palpitating disc, whose every beam,
So keen, so clear, so pure, this living light,
The full resplendence of my planet's star
Singly transcends.   Both heaven and earth I see,
The lovely earth transfigured, it is true,
As when she smileth in a poet's dream,
Or by the golden dawn of love illumed,
That roseate splendour breaking in the east,
Touched with a new and untold loveliness,
A world divine ;—thus glorified appears,
Thus magical, the heaven I now behold,
And so appeared the scenes that met my view,
When from the solemn trance of dreamless death,
Consoled and comforted, in heaven I woke.
But when, on wings of flame, through space we sped
Our system to protect—and when was this ?
Lo, memory serves me not—have years or hours,
In the deep ecstasy of this hushed calm,
Since that high hour elapsed ?—then changed indeed,
This seeming heaven a subtle ether shone,

Enstarred with spirits multitudinous,
That flashed and gleamed through that transpicuous veil,
These visible scenes had vanished from our view.
What is it then this sphere ? Matter or spirit ?
Reality or dream ?

Isis.

Within thyself,
In thine own soul all knowledge is contained ;
The spirit there enthroned all mysteries
Doth comprehend. Fear not to question thou,
That oracle will fail not to reply.
Yet will I speak. The nature thou would'st learn,
The attributes and law of this bright sphere ?
Is it, thou say'st, reality or dream ?
Matter or spirit flame ? And first take note,
Lest those oft-babbled words upon thy lips,
So darkened by the world's philosophies,
And mystified with vain interpretations,
Mislead thee e'en in heaven ; though clear as light.
The outward and the inward, force and form,
Or matter, spirit, terms synonymous
When plainly used and without subtlety,
May not in truth, as thou dost intimate,
Dissevered be ; apart they are not known,

They could not be, do not exist apart ;
'Tis through their union deep and mystical,
And thus alone that being is evolved,
'Tis from that close embrace that life doth spring,
Nature, infinitude, the cosmic whole ;
The poles of being are these principles,
Matter the form which spirit doth assume,
The essence spirit clothed in visible form,
In all created things both manifest,
Reflected each in each, and thus alone,
Thus only recognized ; in world and star,
In these bright spheres and in the conscious soul ;
Of this supernal union the effect
All known phenomena.   But hence 'tis plain,
That in great nature's serial aspects fair,
The true ascent is not from matter gross
To spirit pure ; but from the lower type,
From organisms undeveloped crude,
To higher types ; more subtle complex rare,
Ay to the subtlest most ethereal forms,
Auras intangible and essences,
Magnetic and electric undulations,
Swift light and heat, in all still manifest
The reflex and related attributes

In which the flower of being ever blooms ;
In all the inward thought and outward garb
Related and combined.

Hesperus.

All this is plain,
Thy thought, that gleam divine of living truth,
Within its shadowy veil of flowing words
Clearly I apprehend.

Isis.

The law of life
Of these resplendent, these celestial spheres,
The beaming heavens, on thunder peals of song
And echoing harmonies upborne through space,
Their mystery thou would'st solve.   Have I replied ?
Of pure and occult forces they are wrought,
Irradiate matter, potent, subtle, rare,
Its grosser element inappreciable,
With energies supernal vivified,
And wondrous attributes ; and one of these,
E'en as the mighty ocean's heaving tides
The regnant moon with smile serene controls ;
Or as the trembling needle oscillates

Beneath its guiding star, that they obey,
Submissive to the higher power of mind,
The will collective of their ruling Hosts.
Of transformations magical which seem,
Susceptible, a varied scale sublime
Of visible forms, and which invisible
The measureless infinitudes pervade,
Flashing impalpable from star to star
At our command, winged with the instant gleam
Of viewless thought.   Such mystic qualities,
Inherent in their form and mode of being,
Such glorious and transcendent attributes,
Which from the lower orbs distinguish them,
And render them of these irradiate Hosts
Immutable and free, the blest abode,
Do these fair heavens possess; supernal shrines,
Meet tabernacles of celestial joys
And sacred loves ; where thou wilt ever find
Reality, so called, and seeming one.
This lovely sphere, our home and instrument,
With sensitive vibration tremulous,
Doth to our bidding instantly respond,
As thou hast seen ; our purpose it fulfils,
What we direct, obediently performs,

And, mutable, what we desire appears ;
A fair transfigured globe whereon we dwell,
A potent ether, swift, electrical,
That wafts our gleaming multitudes through space,
Whose flaming breath our thunderbolts transmits ;
Or in the semblance of a floating cloud
Our lovely heaven we know ; whereon serene,
Amid our glowing orbs and clustering worlds,
Invisible we float.

Hesperus.

Ay, there again !
Invisible, and why invisible ?
Why thus denominate these potent spheres,
More splendid far than world-sustaining suns,
And wherefore to the mortals whom we guard,
Conspicuous thus in majesty and grace,
Do we remain unseen ?

Isis.

Nay, 'tis enough
That this effect conditions absolute
And fixed demand, the hierarchal grades
And infinite varieties of souls.
Invisible we are, unseen, unknown,

For those alone whose vision is too dull,
Clouded by fleeting mists and sensual films,
Our pure and radiant presence to detect,
The planet races feebler than ourselves,
With organisms gross with ours compared,
Inferior far in nature and in rank,
And e'en with these, when such is our desire,
Rendered by some great need expedient
A brief suspension of the general law,
In bright and visible form, freely at will,
Communion may we hold.   Ay, in two ways,
To beings all of planetary birth,
The countless orbs of space inhabiting,
May we, angelic, be revealed ; or they,
Themselves ascending in the scale of being,
With inward vision cleansed and purified,
At height of their mortality, the veil
Which held them dark, as well thou know'st, may rend,
And face to face our shining multitudes
In all their pomp behold, or we at need,
Declining to their sad and lower state,
A form transpicuous, more tangible,
In human aspect our effulgence veiled,
As still the higher type the less contains,

May in our turn assume.   This may occur,
Though rarely that sublime prerogative,
Least of the powers with which we move endowed,
For highest ends—a claim exceptional—
Do we exert.   And ever it remains,
That with most people known of planet mould,
In their long processes of change and growth,
The Heavenly Hosts their functions best perform,
The will of the Eterne e'en thus fulfilled,
O'er that vast gulf of severance which divides
Their high and lower states ; which render us
To them invisible.

Hesperus.

Explain no less,
A mystery unsolved since here I walk,
The marvellous resemblance evident
Betwixt the lowly earth and this bright sphere,
These glowing plains and fair terrestrial scenes ;
The glance of recognition, sweet and strange,
Which seems to welcome me where'er I gaze,
Most mystical—a fond familiar smile !
As haply I might mark, might dare discern,
With startled rapture not unmixed with awe,

In the fair countenance of some high guest,
An unknown visitant of lofty mien,
A haunting likeness to a friend beloved
Of humble birth.

Isis.

      This least of all methinks
'Mid mysteries confessed and manifold,
And marvels ever new, within thy mind
Amazement should awake.   One law prevails ;
In every soul, angelical or human,
The higher loveliness enshrined within,
The outward form imperfectly reveals ;
And even so, now on an infinite scale,
Dimly the human races shadow forth
The bright perfection of the Heavenly Hosts,
Through all eternity their prototype
And higher self.   The human life is ours,
All faculties all passions all desires
Inherent in humanity we know ;
The basis of the life angelical,
On which as on a pedestal we stand,
With added powers illimitable crowned,
Wisdom and grace and majesty serene.

For beautiful in bright array we move,
Reflecting in our forms the Soul Eterne,
Supreme o'er accident, and time and change,
By our mood clothed ; by love's keen languor veiled
With roseate gleams soft as a sunset cloud,
Or flaming with the splendours of the day,
Or robed in sacrificial purity
By our own thought ; or by the hour's dread need
Empanoplied for strife.   Free in all ways,
With power at will each semblance to assume
Our purpose that may serve, or, spurning space,
To flash invisible from star to star
Athwart the kingdoms of the Universe ;
So glorious our estate.   And thus, e'en thus,
As we are seen with planet races one,
With those inferior souls our own conjoined,
The heavenly spheres to planets are allied,
A correlation close and intimate,
Fulfilling now in these immense domains,
The vital union of the soul and form,
In all the works of nature manifest ;
Constant in all.   Each phase of loveliness,
Ay, or of terror on thy planet known,
Each aspect by sweet nature there assumed,

Her grand transition, fleeting apparitions,
In storm and calm, in motion and repose,
Phenomenal appearances, no more,
But which reflect sublime realities,
Are shadows of the higher truth of heaven,
The shadow there, here the eternal type,
The semblance there, in heaven the constant form,
There imperfection, here perfection found.
'Tis not then strange that these resplendent scenes
Familiar to thy startled mind should seem,
For this fair sphere is truly of the earth,
The type celestial and ethereal soul,
The earth with added attributes and powers,
Transfigured and divine.

Hesperus.

And these your suns ?

Isis.

Our suns are God.
Ay, yonder lamp our sky illumining,
The lamp of life, star of eternity,
To which with sudden awe expressionless
And wonder deep thy gaze thou dost uplift,
Is very God ; an emanation pure
That from the central source of being flows,

The heaven of heavens, in whose essential flame,
Divinity, on his effulgent throne,
In glory unimaginable reigns ;
The sun of suns, on which all things depend,
Ah ! not of light alone but consciousness,
Round which the glancing systems beautiful,
And throbbing constellations whirl secure
In unremitting flight ; the shrine of Love,
The tabernacle of Omnipotence.
Thus doth His living presence with such smile,
In splendour mild shed through the Universe,
His beaming heavens sustain ; so everywhere,
For as I said in these transcendent spheres
Semblance and blest reality are one,
On each horizon visible appears,
Where'er the glorious angels congregate
And lift to heaven in adoration rapt
Their life-fed gaze.   The mind of the Eterne
In living light thus palpably revealed,
And in this glow of warmth his heart of flame ;
Heaven's light and heat the thought and love of God.

Hesperus.

How then shall I regard those splendid orbs
Which govern the fair planets and control ?

Isis.

Appearances are all phenomena,
The semblance of divine realities,
Necessity of nature is the law,
Freedom the law of the celestial spheres.
The suns that rule the systems physical,
Magnificent, great nature's masterpiece,
Are on that outward and inferior plane
The symbol most sublime of Deity :—
Dread orbs stupendous inconceivable,
Their wandering flocks, their swift and glancing herds,
In safety through the marvellous abyss
Majestical that guide, by law constrained,
Obedient to the central principle
That typifies and symbolizes love,
The gravitating force of living things,
The grasp of atoms and perpetual fall,
The Centre seeking, yearning to the Whole ;
A strong attraction irresistible,
Dread nature's signet of omnipotence,
The wand of power with which she arbitrates
The whirling globes and moving constellations,
As love, the higher law, attracts and guides
All living souls.   Thus are the systems swayed

That tread the orbits of the wilderness.
But free and uncontrolled, the beaming heavens,
By love alone illumed and vivefied,
To their resplendent suns like flowers upturn,
  Those suns whose radiance is the smile of God,
Not seeking thence direction and control,
For all unfettered through the voids they speed,
To no fixed orbit bound or constant path,
As we their blest inhabitants direct,
Impelled and stayed by the collective will
Of their in-dwelling Mind ; not for this cause,
But that ourselves, that we, the radiant Hosts,
In heaven supreme—O life, and highest bliss !
Rapture known only in Eternity !—
Fed at the fount of Being Infinite,
The source exhaustless of Essential Love,
Should evermore the smile of God reflect,
And in his sight rejoice.

Hesperus.

   Night, ye know not ?
Or so I deem, for since in heaven I walk,
The holy sun of love has ever shone,
Seeming in its majestic course to star
An endless day ?

c

Isis.

Thou errest Hesperus.
For said I not that all things known on earth
Are here alone in full perfection found.
That mild beneficence, with starry front,
Or sphered imperial with her satellite,
Who beareth gently on her hovering wing,
On earth so well beloved, so fondly wooed,
And wooed how oft in vain, soft brooding sleep ;
Her breast, the holy refuge of distress,
Her breath the dewy balm renewing life,
Sweet night we know ; not to this realm denied,
Her passive joys and negative delights.
A night divine, beyond thy utmost dream
How ravishing ; but free as is our day,
For less to us this season of repose,
Than to sense-fettered, frail humanities,
And all too full our life of ardent claims
And joys, to be oft veiled in pensive dream ;
Whence is our night by no fixed seasons bound,
But subject to our call and our command,
Our sun evanishing at our desire,
And beaming in new aspect from on high,

Now in the congregated stars beheld,
Or golden splendour of a mild-eyed moon,
Then when in twilight's dim and mystic streams,
Activity suspended, we would lave,
Or quaff at midnight strength and life renewed,
From fountains dark and fragrant of repose ;
A night of hours succeeding a long day
Of months perchance ; or years, or centuries ;
We know not time, to us eternity,
We know not space—all space our present state.

Hesperus.

Thus evermore we live, by night and day,
Encompassed by the consciousness of God ?

Isis.

Ay, evermore, through all the endless years.
With each warm glance of yon resplendent orb,
Each star-beam faint, or interlunar ray,
The will of God, eternal and divine,
In radiance flashed on our responsive minds,
Is perfectly to every soul revealed ;—
With every breath of this auroral air,
His love, his life, his consciousness, we breathe,

And hence in heaven the Will Supreme is known,
And hence in Heaven is everywhere obeyed.
What wouldst thou more ?

Hesperus.

My mind still hovering floats
Insatiate of the truth, with brooding thought,
O'er the sweet mystery of heaven and earth.
Since each fair planet in her airy flight
Companioned whirls with her immortal star,
The heavens themselves, in their resplendent ranks,
No less so than the systems they protect,
Which strew with glittering archipelagoes
The silent gulfs and amplitudes of space,
Must be, they too, countless, innumerous ;
And like those orbs varied in rank and type.

Isis.

All nature's serial forms are infinite
In all her fruitful kingdoms and domains.
The fields of space, e'en as by solar groups,
By these ethereal spheres are strewn and thrilled,
As manifold ; nor less in their bright ranks,
The chiefest law of form, variety,

As constancy of spirit is the law,
Do they display.   In every system known,
Both heavens and worlds a grand career fulfil,
Both immaterial and material orbs,
Revealing one same form of loveliness,
Governed by one fair star in many groups;
Or dual majesties, or monarch orbs
More numerous, in splendour intricate
And state combined.   The type which each presents
In its divine completeness is beheld
In heaven alone, while in the lower worlds,
According to their state 'tis reproduced,
With relative identity and truth;
In some reflected in faint hues appears,
Or, it may be, distorted shows and marred,
In others boldly limned with grace and power
As in a mirror shines.   Lo, everywhere,
Around us, o'er us, 'neath us, far and near,
Their splendours irridescent flash and gleam,
And ever, as the radiant scale ascends,
More marvellous they glow and palpitate,
More subtly beautiful, more pure and rare,
Until, with flower-like grace, the central heavens,
Their shining ranks unfold; where, beatific,

Veiled in the glory of essential light,
The loftiest spirits known, in awful pomp
And incommunicable ecstasy,
Where these abide—flamelike Resplendences,
The holy Cherubim and Seraphim,
And dread Archangels, in superb array,
Whose dazzling groups and intricate involve,
Like keen and throbbing stars, the throne Eterne,
His secret counsels with High God who share,
Who execute His ultimate commands,
And guard inscrutable the lower Hosts,
As in their turn these Hosts the planets realms
Guide and control; supreme in loveliness,
Wisdom and love, and laved in mystic joys,
All thought, all dream beyond; e'en to ourselves
Unknown and unrevealed.

Hesperus.

This sphere divine,
But that I need not ask, guards and protects
The lowly orb where first I drew life-breath,
My mother earth.

Isis.

Ay, truly, 'tis our charge,

A mote obscure, unnoted, unremarked,
Which throbs and whirls 'mid splendours numberless
That far transcend her undistinguished flame ;
One grain of sand on the eternal shore,
And yet by us, her guardians, well beloved.
Freely we wander 'mid the realms of space,
And many orbs, as thou hast seen, protect,
But to that globe alone by sacred ties
Indissoluble an allied, one thought,
One dream incarnate of the Mind Supreme.
The human souls who on that planet dwell,
When by their lofty faculties prepared
The higher life celestial to attain,
And freed in their last pilgrimage by death,
To this bright sphere ascend ; here joyful quaff,
By Love presented with seraphic smile,
The golden cup of immortality,
Here find their haven of eternal rest,
Their everlasting home.   Nor for ourselves,
Within the azure realm of endless day,
The fields of light and song, can we, in truth,
A loftier place of more distinction claim.
This glorious sphere, our home, our shrine, our
    heaven,

No higher rank 'mid heavenly orbs maintains,
Than 'mid the planets of the Universe
In all her insignificance the earth ;
Herein between the two, as in all things,
A correspondence close discernable,
Most intimate.

Hesperus.

Nay, pause, my spirit quails.
A shadow vague and dim, intangible,
Cast us 'twould seem by our own happiness,
The night inorbing this seraphic day—
O, dread to be endured—on my soul falls.
The insignificance of earth, ah, that indeed
I might admit, but not of this fair sphere ;
How contemplate, how e'en conceive that thought ?
Where heaven is thus regarded, what am I ?
One feeble spark of glimmering consciousness ;
One soul by her own nothingness o'erwhelmed ;
My senses reel.

Isis.

Such words in our fair courts,
Young Hesperus, a strange discordant note
Unwonted strike—such words are blasphemy.

'Tis through our knowledge of the Infinite,
And thus alone, our contemplation rapt
And comprehension of the central Mind,
That our dependent minds are self-revealed.
In this abyss plunges the finite soul,
And from its solemn depths emerges calm,
O not with her own weakness now dismayed,
But winged with power; of her exalted state,
Her import and inate divinity,
Now first aware. In that unfathomed sea,
Whose breaking billows bright are constellations,
In whose star-flecked immensity this heaven
And countless love-enkindled shrines as fair,
Are truly less than tiny drops of rain
That twinkle on a river's broad expanse
And disappear; spaceless, illimitless,
Which all the blazing systems gem-bestrewn,
With light and life and loveliness pervade,
And yet fill not with all their glancing fires,
The ocean of eternity, of God,
Therein all things, each heaven, each world, each star,
And how much more the temples fair of thought,
All living souls, both human and angelic,
A grandeur strange and mystical assume,
Loom up, e'en in their insignificance,

Divine ; for in that dread infinitude
The measurements of finite beings fail,
And throb those mental atoms scintillant,
Which, as the morning's smile a drop of dew,
Reflect in countless forms the Mind Eterne,
In cadence with the universal pulse ;
The life in all is kindled at one source,
The quickening breath, the spirit-flame is God ;
In thy young breast, nerved with angelic strength,
And in the mortal frail whom thou dost guard,
And, light-ensphered, in those bright Seraphim,
On thee who shed, with calm beneficence,
Their beaming smile.   All beings are allied,
And Deity in every heart enthroned,
Most solemn thought ; and hence on that broad plane,
Viewed from the stand-point of the Absolute,
There were the mystic circle rounds itself,
Fulfilled in fleeting time Eternity,
And in all finite forms the Infinite,
All equal are and one.

Hesperus.

A glorious thought,
And true, in promise and fruition true,

In mine own heart I feel the throbbing pulse,
'That in all living creatures palpitates,
In mine own veins the glowing tide I feel,
Which flowing from the unexhausted Source,
All souls, all beings in the Universe,
Unites, and with his spirit animates ;
The tide essential, pure, of Deity,
Eternal, uncreated, unrevealed,
The Absolute

Isis.

    Bear then that thought in mind,
Nor speak again in thy resplendent home,
The breath inhaling of this fragrant air,
Illumined by the smile of yonder sun,
Of thy soul's nothingness. On what new theme
Wouldst hold discourse ?

Hesperus.

    Whence do they come, these spheres ?
'These beaming heavens ? how first originate ?
How breathed ecstatic forth in glorious form ?
And whence the lesser lights o'er which they brood,
The whirling systems of terrestrial orbs,
Whose radiant groups they shelter and protect ?

The origin of all things I would know,
That mystery profound, inscrutable,
From human apprehension and desire
So darkly veiled.

Isis.

To thee no mystery.
At heart of the great truths e'en now declared
The knowledge thou dost seek resplendent glows.

Hesperus.

And yet more perfectly and in detail,
Thou, with thy living word, those subtle truths
Help me to penetrate.

Isis.

Most marvellous
The ceaseless plying of the web of being
And most divine.   In nature's kingdoms vast,
One constant law as well thou kuow'st obtains.
The pulse that beats within each mortal frame
Is hymn of life and knell of swift decay :
Death feeds on life, and from his dark embrace
Successive forms emerge of purer type,
Ascending still, 'till in these radiant realms

The gloomy monarch of the shadowy tomb,
Consumed by immortality, is slain ;
To love transformed.   Thy present aspect fair,
The outward shape of light and majesty
Which thy ethereal spirit has assumed,
Irradiate sprang quick from thy mortal mould,
By thine own thoughts evolved, thy deeds and words,
Impalpable emotions and desires,
More potent forces than blind mortals deem,
Weaving in ceaseless free activity,
Thus subtly wrought in thy terrestrial life,
Thy soul's immortal garb.   And thou new born,
In thy celestial, thy supernal state,
To thy less favoured race with patient love
Wilt minister.   But man is nature's mirror,
And in this process clearly may be traced
The larger movements and vicissitudes
Of all created things.   And thus, in truth,
The orbs magnificent whereof we spoke,
The central suns of planetary realms
Not only rule their whirling vassal trains,
But in their progress through unending time
And viewless space, as their own life decays,
Their force material wastes and dissipates—

For e'en these monarch orbs begin and end,
Are born and die, fulfilling nature's law,
Although indeed in times that endless seem,
Durations vast—the lovely heavens evolve,
Themselves eternal suns of grander type,
Ay, feed and nourish them with splendid smile,
The everflowing waves of light and heat, .
The glowing beams and ardent palpitations,
Which by their planet kingdom unconsumed
Stream forth in vacancy and there seem lost ;
But which, far otherwise, for ends supreme,
For service high and ultimate reserved,
Are by these spheres arrested in their course,
Attracted by these magnets of the voids,
And fitted subtlest substance to sustain—
So pure and potent those sidereal beams—
In their bright woof absorbed.   But these fair heavens
Are shrines of love where dwell the Hosts Divine,
Who, in their course, terrestrial systems guard,
And on the whirling planets watchful shed
The spirit germs from whence immortal spring
All sentient forms.

Hesperus.

Vast system and sublime !

Which in its grand, inwrought simplicity,
And sequence logical, a child might grasp.
E'en on the ignorant earth science reveals
That naught in nature is, or can be, lost ;
High truth which feeble mortals venerate,
And prate thereof, while failing in their folly,
The sacred law which they themselves proclaim,
In its relations infinite, to trace :
Too narrow in their scope to apprehend
Its absolute immutable perfection,
Most constant, poised, and irreversible.
But pause not thou.   Say on.

Isis.

What more remains ?
Methought e'er this thy query had been solved.
In every being crowned with consciousness,
Body and soul, indissolubly linked,
Appear, dependent ever each on each.
And in all living things this twofold form
Exists ; each system of terrestrial orbs
With its celestial system is allied,
Each through their union known and manifest.
Terrestrial races, in their countless ranks,

Inert and apathetic, would pass away,
If by the ethereal races unsustained,
Their purer self and living prototype,
Whose lovelier forms they fugitive reflect,
And in the consummation of their course
To whom ascend. The glittering constellations,
With all their whirling orbs bespangling space,
Extinguished would dissolve, in chaos lost,
In night and silence unapparent perish,
If to those throbbing lights innumerous
The spheres celestial failed in their response,
Their purer counterparts ; which, swift and free,
As in the human frame the subtle nerves
Transmit to every part with instant gleam
The will and motions of the conscious mind,
But for that vital tracery extinct,
A fleshly bulk inanimate and cold,
Through nature's realms the glowing messages,
And word of being flash.

Hesperus.

    Nay pause not thus.
I hang enchanted on the flowing stream
Of thy seraphic strain.

Isis.

Each solar realm
A purer realm celestial doth sustain,
Each heaven to its own planet is attached,
The lower world in whose reflected forms
And semblances the type is shadowed forth,
Which all unclouded in perfection pure,
The higher sphere displays; and which for aye,
With life and spirit flame it animates.
The heavenly Hosts, who people these fair shrines,
The safety of their orbs dependent guard,
The living souls who dwell therein protect,
And joyful greet in their celestial home,
When immortality, life's highest meed,
And virtue's final and supreme reward,
They purified attain; blest human souls,
The consecrated spirits from below
Swift-speeding to recruit these shining ranks
Left vacant in their turn by spirits pure
Upsoaring hence to still diviner realms;
For progress is our law no less than man's,
And through eternity, flame-palpitant,
The stream of souls regenerate ascends,

D

From world to heaven, and from each starry sphere
To brighter heavens beyond.   Spirit and form,
In nature's evanescent forms revealed,
In every realm united are beheld,
As closely linked, the Seen and the Unseen,
In glowing systems of responsive orbs,
As frame and essence in each conscious soul,
And in like mode indissolubly bound,
The body of the universe and mind :
Through endless time their mystical embrace
Shown forth in its effect, and that creation ;
Each pole by its related pole evolved,
Each realm by its responsive realm evoked,
Without beginning hence, and endless hence,
Throughout eternity the living Spirit,
The all-pervading Consciousness Supreme,
Still in this twofold semblance manifest ;
Thus seen, thus known, in all created things,
Minute and infinitesimal each atom,
And vast, illimitable, infinite,
The cosmic Whole ; in planctury tribes
And beaming o'er them the Angelic Hosts,
The animated Universe of Mind,
And in the whirling systems numberless,

With their related and resplendent spheres;
The Kosmos in its aspect physical;
Spirit and form in all the type of being,
And God of all supernal, absolute,
The life and soul.   Thy problem is resolved,
Of the origin of things no more is known;
No more than this, no more can be revealed,
Though by the subtlest Essences Supreme,
Whose beatific and resplendent ranks
The throne Eternal guard.

Hesperus.

Transcendent hour.
In all its scope thy thought at last I seize,
Thy meaning apprehend.   A flame divine,
From yonder orb magnificent shed down,
E'en like a blessing on my brow descends,
Unspeakable, a pure and hallowing gleam,
The smile transfiguring of holy Love,
All heaven by that effulgence is illumed,
While mine own mind enkindled and aroused,
With faculties and judgment vivified,
The sacred heart of nature penetrates,
The problems dark and mysteries obscure

That e'en in heaven perplexed and baffled me,
Discerning at a glance and solving them ;
Beholding all unveiled, with vision clear,
Truth's countenance. With glow of vigorous life,
And strength divine unknown until this hour,
Ay, unimagined e'en in heaven itself,
Flower-like, in this celestial atmosphere,
My soul expands.

Isis.

So will it ever be.
Each hour of bliss in this ethereal sphere,
New lustre to thy heavenly grace will add,
Thy power augment, insight intensify.
Each smile of yonder orb, beneficent,
Thy mind with higher wisdom will imbue,
Each breath inhaled of this celestial air,
Thy nature quicken and inspire. For lo,
Each ray emitted by the Sun of Truth
Tells of its origin—the soul supreme ;
While unto thee belongs and appertains
A mind of apprehension infinite,
Wherewith in blissful contemplation rapt,
Through all the seasons of recurrent time,

The æons and the ages yet to be,
Those everflowing beams and living rays
To scrutinize.   With golden raptures winged,
In each joy-freighted hour of every day
That dawns upon thee in thy blest estate,
In the grand volume of celestial lore,
With joy and dread new problems shalt thou solve,
New truths profound discern in every page,
And depths profound of meaning apprehend,
In thy inferior state all unconceived,
In facts already known ; advancing still,
More true, more beautiful, more wise each day ;
Ascending still ; more noble, god-like, pure ;
All this thy heavenly life shall verify.
But the great truths, immutable, sublime,
In this high hour to thy young mind revealed,
Unchanged shall these abide for evermore,
Constant remain through all eternity ;—
The fundamental principles of life,
The underlying axioms of things,
Of nature and of soul.   These central laws
At once and with clear vision must thou grasp,
Nor lose thereon thy hold, for lo ! thereon
The Universe doth stand.

Hesperus.

One question more.

Isis.

Not so, nay truly, I deny thy prayer.
Enough of solemn converse and debate;
How then, the heart of all philosophy,
Like honey dew, in one sweet hour wouldst quaff,
Bee-like enamoured thus? Nay, let us hence,
And seek mid other scenes companionship,
And pleasures new. O'erwrought with life intense,
With high events and immemorial strife,
Too passionate have throbbed the ardent hours
Of thy brief sojourn in this heavenly sphere.
Thou know'st not yet, dream'st not, young Hesperus,
What new delights, in rich variety,
Like plenteous flowers sown on a fragrant sward,
Await thy life to crown. Star-like on earth,
Already known to thee through their great works,
And deathless fame, the Spirits of the past,
Whom thou, on that low sphere, didst venerate,
Feeding at their full fount thy younger stream,
Thy worshipped Masters and thy Guides so late,

These shall we seek in majesty enthroned ?
Their benediction wilt thou claim and hail ?
And whom wilt thou select ?   I read thy heart !
Thy country's peerless poet well-beloved,
Thy Dante with his laurel'd brow severe,
And Michael Angelo, that Titan soul,
God-like mid gods who walks in heavenly fields,
Whose awful name, in living characters
Emblazoned on thy cities monuments,
Shall worshipped be while time endures.   'Tis well.
No strangers wilt thou find that mighty twain.
They knew and loved thee in thy human form,
Thy mortal course with interest observed,
And oft, in that swift glancing pilgrimage,
Too soon arrested for man's sake and cause,
Eclipsed in that sad hour thy planet's star,
With holy ministrations visited,
A young disciple treading in their steps.
Hence, to my guidance trust.

Hesperus.

Nay, gentle Isis,
Those holy Seraphim, in heaven enthroned,
And in my heart of hearts, there worshipped still,

Who once the earth they dwelt upon transformed,
Not in this hour, sublime with other claims,
With love and reverence in heavenly courts,
Empassioned may I seek.   A vain desire,
For hapless souls now dwelling on that earth,
By wrong assailed, in grief, anxiety,
My strong protection instantly demand,
My aid implore.   Vittoria's voice I hear,
Her human cry sobs on the pitying air
With plaintive wail ; and at that soft appeal,
As when a mother o'er her offspring yearns,
Her youngest born, in danger and alarm,
With tenderness divine and sympathy,
My yearning soul is moved.   Lo, I must hence.
When I return in some sweet hour serene,
Fulfilment of thy promise claiming then,
Thy guidance to those regal souls I'll seek ;
But now the earth demands me—must receive—
Thither on wings of thought and love I speed,
So for this while farewell.

Scene II.—*The same. Sudden access of light and movement in the heavenly sphere. Enter Hyperion and Aglaia.*

Hyperion.

Hail, Isis sweet !—who vanished thus from view,
At our approach ?   An instant seen and lost,
Like some swift, shooting star engulphed in space.
Young Hesperus was't not ?

Isis.

Ay, Hesperus.
A pleading cry, Vittoria's voice be heard,
And at the summons sped with swift response
To meet her claim ; nor this his first essay
In his new task of moulding that young soul,
And guiding on her shadowed path obscure.
But what occurs in these resplendent courts ?
What startling and most glad intelligence,
Stirs thus our radiant Hosts ?

Hyperion.

In truth, great news,
A convocation has been summoned forth
Of potent spheres, to meet in radiant pomp,
And witness a momentous festival
Soon on the planet Mira to be held,
Whose youthful race their apogee attain;
Our benediction on that favoured orb
And people to bestow.

Isis.

Sweet, flower-like globe.
How oft in pensive meditation rapt,
O'er her transcendent and most varied scenes,
And happy peoples in their youthful pride
Delighted I have hung; there pondering
The high achievement of their guardian Host,
A barren world who rescued from her fate,
And to a glowing Paradise transformed,
Ruled by a peerless race, and efflorescent
In ceaseless bloom.   From our celestial groups,
No whirling splendour 'mid the gems of space,
A truer interest more profound can claim,
For none exists in all essential points

More like our own more humble planet charge,
Although indeed sweet Mira's rarer gifts
On that inferior orb are latent still,
And by her manifold defects obscured.
But what thy equanimity disturbs?
Nay, speak, Hyperion fair, what troubles thee,
And darkens thus thy brow?

Aglaiæ.

Need'st thou demand,
When our poor earth in misery and wrath
Is groaning thus undone? Her sad estate,
The wreck of noble hopes, e'en while we speak,
Betrayed. O infamy beyond belief!
The fall of Rome, the sacrificial stream
Which from the breast of bleeding Paris flows,
The devastation of the hearts we love,
All this, methinks, for sorrow on our part,
Regret and pain, might prove sufficient cause.

Hyperion.

Ay, all goes wrong in that ungrateful world,
Rome sombre sits, dethroned and desolate,
Her new-born hopes in gloomy midnight quenched,

Her freedom lost, o'errun, defeated, chained,
As in some early age, of foreign troops
The vanquished prey.   Mazzini, her brave chief
Struck down from his high place is driven forth,
Exiled, forlorn, while his victorious foe,
The French Republic's faithless President,
And Emperor foresworn—a fit exchange—
Of that distracted land the destined bane,
And of all Europe at this hour the curse,
Completes his work.   On fallen Rome he stands,
And drawing deadly strength from her defeat,
His crimson hand unhallowed stretches forth,
And plunges deep, a foul and treacherous blow,
From which far greater evils than appear
And wrongs will spring, in his own country's breast ;
A deed remorseless, cruel to the core,
And barbed unhappily with full success,
Which perfectly Napoleon's end attains,
For while unhappy Paris 'wildered stands,
Silent through sheer amazement and dismay,
His restless throne, rocked on the vengeful blood
Of her pure patriots and illustrious sons,
His friends erewhile, companions, brothers sworn,
Unhindered he ascends.   A swift descent,

Progress in every state in Europe checked,
This triumph and mischance deplorable,
Ill-omened, on the steep and downward path,
The headlong precipice of retrogression
Establishes. For this false Emperor—
Although the end uncertain still remains
Of the dark epoch by his reign begun,
Of lawless violence—so much is plain,
The master of the hour henceforth confessed,
Trading upon the glory of a name,
Will stamp his brazen signet on the time,
And this most servile generation bend,
Magniloquent with futile aspirations,
Desires corrupt and false philanthropies,
Cringing to wear his hateful livery,
And in its own defeat disgrace and shame
Most harlot-like rejoice.

Isis.

Unfortunate,
Reserved a sombre pageant to adorn,
A sad and dark career awaiting him,
He dreams his dream, and in a dangerous place.
I pity him, and blame in fact, no more,
Than some sleep-walker in his heavy trance.

His mind is dull and weak, sluggish at best,
And full of dreams fantastic, and desires.
His power, 'tis true, rests solely on his name,
But though all France, and Europe far and wide,
That potent name, a true magician's wand,
Has charmed or cowed   (O, foolish nations all,
Despite your ripe maturity and power,
By such vain baubles to be led astray)—
He too by his own magic is beguiled ;
Of fortune thinks himself the favoured son,
Selected by the Powers Unseen, marked out,
To play the rôle of a great Emperor—
A rôle too oft pathetic in these days,
And he a figure tragical therein—
Deems this his God-appointed destiny ;
Imagines o'er his fated head a star
That shines alone in his sick fantasy,
The ignis-fatuus of a morbid brain,
Illusive quite.   Passive and cold, inert,
A tyrant he is not, or would not be,
Without a tyrant's strength or energy,
If to his nature true, unlike in this
The founder of his line, whose strong right arm,
Whose giant intellect and iron will,

A despot's right divine, upreared the throne
Whereon he sat a thunder-bolt of war,
His daring crimes by noble deeds redeemed,
Wise acts and righteous laws.   Not so this man,
Irresolute, who wanders forth in dream
On dangerous heights unsuited to his tread.
Ay, though he wades to his unhallowed throne
Through blood, a sacred stream of forfeit life,
That from his hand flows forth to purple waste,
That blood itself, in half unconsciousness,
In ignorance of the dread forfeiture,
Was blindly shed.   He knows not what he does.
The deadliest deeds demanded by his rôle,
To him appear, sad thought, mere sacrifice.
An object of compassion most profound,
We can but pity him, this I repeat;
For some most abject fall this blood-stained triumph,
Disgrace world-wide and endless infamy,
Must in the end repay.   His fate is sealed;
While France, though sorely wounded by his blow,
And doomed to be corrupted by his reign,
Too well prepared, alas! for her disease,
Will from that slow prostration spring renewed,
Such strength, such youthful vigour in her lies,

He cannot stay the ocean's swelling tide,
Or time's swift flight retard.

Hyperion.

'Tis true, I grant ;
And yet his sensual reign, slothful and base,
May mark the turning of that tide, and does.
It may, sad thought, the highest point denote,
Which this irresolute and feeble race,
Arrested in their course and onward march,
Will e'er attain.

Isis.

Rather himself shall prove
Our instrument ; this too is in his rôlè.
For is he not the soldier of the future ?
Is not his watchword progress, and his star ?
Is't not in freedom's name and for her sake
That his cold steel has struck her bleeding breast ?
The vital truths that to the age belong,
The sacred laws determining of nations,
The rights inherent of the struggling peoples,
And of their rulers the inherent rights,
And many voiced, insisting urgently

That holy peace forthwith established be,
Upon a sure foundation, that of law ;
These great momentous questions of the hour,
The principles to be with power proclaimed
By all who love mankind ; through which alone
The next great step of progress can be made,
On which the welfare of the race depends,
He vaguely comprehends, grant him his due,
Their force he feels, sees their necessity,
And to associate seeks with their success,
Though for a selfish end, his name and fame.
What more can we desire, our part is plain.
Aid him his hopeful purpose to achieve,
Ay, give him way ; good service he will render.
Let this be his appointed work.   'Twill live,
The evil that he does, the wrong he wreaks,
Will like a cloud rack pass.

Hyperion.

Too much to hope.
Those thoughts are all pervading in the air,
The Spirit of the Age has quickened them,
And on their prompt solution now insists.
No statesman lives, 'mid those at least of mark,

E

Whose heads upon their shoulders fairly rest,
And are not turned awry, seeking the past,
Who fearless the great future dare confront,
With level gaze sublime ; 'mid these are none
Who fail to apprehend and recognize,
Of these momentous problems of the hour,
Most pressing and most formidable,
Brought forward by the swift development,
The rapid growth organic of the race,
By this mere fact thrust into prominence,
The urgent claim.   Ay, e'en this Bonaparte,
This King of Shadows, Emperor of Shams,
In the dull mirror of his turbid brain,
Some gleam of that wide-spreading day reflects,
Though faint and dim.   But build not thou thereon.
Nothing of good shall flow from that base source,
No aid from him, though in his own despite,
Be wrested ever in a sacred cause.
To fortify his most uncertain throne,
He must perforce assume, for his own sake,
The peoples and the nations to defend :
Must seek the Champion to appear of law,
Of progress, order, magnanimity,
But to the last his pledge will be betrayed,

As by the first act it has been betrayed,
Of his unworthy reign, which he begins
By trampling down with ruthless violence
The holy torch of freedom in two lands.
For 'twas through him alone that Rome was crushed,
And his own country now, in her new hope,
Lies bleeding 'neath his blow.

Isis.

Ah, it is true.
And yet upon an Emperor's lips mere words,
Though by his life and actions falsified,
Have oft, full oft, truth's messages proclaimed,
So readily the masses are beguiled,
With power reverberating far and wide,
Clothed with authority. 'Tis sad indeed.
We hoped too much from these slow-moving peoples,
And for some while in sweet illusions lapped,
Now waken from our dream. The era new,
Of freedom, of prosperity and peace,
Demanded by their ripe development,
Which should have been in this triumphant hour
Their conquest for all time, by luxury
And lust betrayed, they bitterly forsake ;

E 2

From their true path with scarce a struggle turn,
And, retrograde, in their old quagmires sink
Of anarchy and crime.   Most ominous,
An era of reaction, dark and drear,
Of faithless selfishness and unbelief,
And shameful greed begins.   So let it be.
Ay, let them have their wars, bleed at each vein,
Sink in a sea of wide-spread misery
Whose waves are blood.   Stern lessons they will learn,
And in a century or so perchance,
Through sorrow and defeat at last prepared
The future in its glory to confront,
Will once again the Holy Temple seek—
That sacred shrine—of harmony and peace,
From which they now have swerved.

Hyperion.

'Tis possible.
Yet do I hold it folly, nothing less,
Mere sentimental weakness to assume,
Although such optimism, I confess,
A soothing influence on the mind exerts,
That of necessity from evil thus,
Good forfeited will spring.   If this were all

The danger I foresaw, some years of strife,
Needed in preparation by the race,
To fit them for a future more assured,
I should not thus my voice lift in complaint.
'Tis not the case.   For truly to my mind
A thousand dangerous symptoms indicate
That this relapse of energy and faith
May prove a permanent decline ; a waste
For which no renovation will be found.
For 'tis not now as when mankind was young ;
Events march quickly in this latter day,
And now a year outweighs a century,
Ay, many centuries, it oft may prove,
Of æons immature.   In Europe now,
Where throbs with painful throes the world's large
    heart,
A certain stage of ripe development,
Has been attained ; the peoples there are one ;
Their voices they uplift in one same prayer,
And if they fail ere long to apprehend
The new conditions of the time and hour,
Which their organic unity demands,
Thus blind if they should prove, their doom is sealed,
Defeat henceforth will mark their baffled course ;

The present grade to which with slow ascent,
With doubt and anguished travail they have climbed,
How far beneath the height that lured their hope,
Will prove the sun-lit summit of their march.
From whence their downward path will darkly lead,
With every step more stormily beset,
Dogged and bewildered by the wars and woes
On which so lightly now headlong they rush,
The realm of chaos and fierce anarchy,
Confusion worse confounded.   And in that case,
We all are well aware on what blank rock
Their shattered bark will break.

Isis

                Ay, then no doubt,
The skill we should be forced to emulate
Of that grand Host who guard beneficent
The very orb of which we now discoursed,
And shall erewhile with benediction seek,
Mira, that lovely globe ;—sweep them away,
As they some ages since—a dread exploit !
Dealt with the recreant and unhappy race
Who on that planet their high hope betrayed.
Abandon them to their more mournful fate,

Some dread catastrophe world-wide permit,
Or e'en induce; an inundation vast,
Or conflagration kindled from on high,
Which would alas! in its remorseless course
Mankind destroy; when, free and unrestrained,
Through certain changes in its structure wrought,
The globe itself, so desert now and rude,
We grandly might renew; there fashion forth
A glowing shrine of happiness and love
For loftier peoples meet.

Aglaia.

Ah, say not so.
Clothe not with vital breath a thought so sad,
Send not that ominous suggestion forth,
To quicken in the atmosphere new thought,
And thus for its own dread accomplishment
Perchance prepare.   No, no, suggest it not!
The lovely earth whose plains ourselves have trod,
And with our tears bedewed; the suffering race
From whose large veins our own, as from a fount,
Drew first their life.

Hyperion.

The race would still survive,
Although these peoples perished that would live,
And live conspicuous in a higher type,
For this at least our skill responsible ;
A peerless flower perchance of mortal mould,
In whom true satisfaction we might find,
Our hope deferred and long enduring faith
At last well justified. For these poor worms,
In crawling swarms now battening on the soil,
So they have named themselves and are no more,
With some few bright exceptions, I admit,
But all too few to leaven the dull mass,
They weary me ; impatient I have grown
With their delays and doubts and hesitations,
Their self delusions, guile, hypocrisy ;
It angers me with all that has been done
To lead them upward to a higher path,
To see them still thus cleaving to the dust,
Impracticable, blind. Ay, for my part,
'Twould not, I own it, lacerate my soul,
To greet our globe in her impetuous course,
And check with some imperative salute,

A tap on her frost-fettered, polar brow,
Or clasp unloving of her torrid zone,
Which might perchance, nay, would with certainty,
The countless tribes that now her plains infest,
Those myrmidons lost to the higher truth,
Exterminate. The blow would be deserved,
And that stern blow, undaunted, to inflict,
Will prove, or soon or late, I scarce can doubt,
Our wisest course.

Aglaia.

Nay, this is mockery,
Or thou thyself art most unjust, unwise.
Poor peoples much abused—ne'er till this age
Could they have satisfied our present claim,
Too undeveloped still and unallied
The members of the body politic
To comprehend their true associate form,
And shall no respite now be granted them,
No further day of grace for vacillation,
Doubt and defeat ? Then we should be their scourge ;
For 'tis too high a race to be o'erthrown,
Despite their sad and terrible defects,
Which may with time eradicated be,

And surely will, if we are faithful found,
If we lose not our courage, patience, hope,
Ay, and o'er all for those unhappy souls,
Our heart-felt love.

Hyperion.

Nay, fear not sweet Aglaia,
Our patience will not fail while hope in them
Exists ; but let them not delay too long.
Twelve men in Europe now, e'en as of old,
Twelve fishermen they claim transformed the world,
So now to-day twelve men of rank and power,
Of virtue and authority—for this,
All strengths combined this age demands—with brain
The issues of the time to comprehend,
And will to carry them in prompt effect,
Twelve centuries of strife might save the world,
And it may be with their sole voice prevent
A permanent decline.   Europe to-day,
As his small plot of ground a husbandman
Renews and fructifies with patient toil,
They with consummate skill might recreate.
The masses everywhere, rude as they seem,
For vast ameliorations are prepared,

They scent their hope and pant for their new life.
And if their rightful claims were recognized,
The nationalities, that principle,
With all that it includes, forthwith avowed,
And law and order in all lands proclaimed,
Established their supreme authority,
The living rock impregnable, whereon
The temple of sweet peace might be upreared,
That one sole change, one step, a single one,
Would save them and redeem.   Secure henceforth,
From discord and diplomacy set free,
To be by justice ruled and common sense,
Howe'er or in what form administered,
Would matter not, all governments divine,
Adapted each the welfare to promote,
Of some one branch of the great family,
The peoples and their rulers, one at heart,
By that transition most sublime assured
Their mutual claims, would mutually be blessed ;
And those harmonious sister states, allied,
A happy federation, confident,
Their true career begin.   The armies huge
Which now their rich vitality exhaust,
E'en like a spectral nightmare would dissolve,

And on their wreck, with efflorescence swift,
An era unexampled, glorious,
On science reared, illustrious in art,
Most gracious bloom.   The fetters of the past,
The false philosophies and creeds corrupt,
By which the intellect of the whole race
Is clogged and bound, as of themselves would fall,
And each new step demanded by their growth,
Clearly discerned in that effulgent day,
Would be securely taken ; a grand ascent,
Thick-strewn with proud discoveries and joys.
Then in brief time, a century perchance,
With what more god-like gifts this race, our charge,
Would prove endowed, to what transcendent heights
They might aspire, what fruitful kingdoms win,
We safely could pronounce ; assured to all,
For this at least at once might be assumed,
On earth a noble and serene career,
The happy threshold of a life divine,
Their final goal.   Twelve men might do all this !
'Tis all too slight a claim.   By one alone,
One energetic, one devoted soul,
Of daring genius, intellect and will,
And duly by authority sustained,

All this might be achieved ; so subtly true,
So sensitive in its response has grown
To each new influence and high appeal,
With all its living, thinking particles,
Its individualized, atomic minds
In action and full play, the general Mind ;
So formed erewhile and conscious has become
The universal Soul.   The way is clear,
And one strong effort might the goal attain :
But if the race develope not ere long
Sufficient force wise leaders to produce,
And in the quickened masses to evolve
A higher virtue than they yet have shown,
That so their leaders they may aptly choose,
And their great minds when these appear obey—
For now the spring is loud and in the tree
The sap should rise and vigorous shoots put forth—
Perish it will ; condemned not by this Host,
But by offended law ; slain by truth's sword,
The just reward of ignorance and sloth,
And incapacity.

Isis.

If they shall fail,

When all is said, their new life to evolve,
A higher era blest inaugurate,
How sad will be the thought, most hard to bear,
To their deliverance that they stood so near ;
Nay, they will find their courage yet, doubt not ;
Catch from the echoing stars the word of fate,
And their divine inheritance secure :
In many nations hopeful signs I see.

Aglaia.

From England I hope much.

Hyperion.

    A sad mistake.
From England 'mid the nations least of all
In this new age of strife and vital change,
Is room for hope.   I dread her influence.
A marplot she, and drag on fortune's wheel,
Without one cause her folly to excuse.
Henceforth her boundless strength will naught avail,
Good impulses and aptitudes sincere,
Her power and wealth, advantages immense
Which o'er all other nations she enjoys,

For insight she has not, nor faith ideal,
The leaven lacks of living principle.
She all too long has been content to find
In mere material gain her happiness,
In ceremonial forms her chiefest good,
And this the consequence.   Ay, thou shalt see.
That strong-hewed bulk, those sinews firmly knit,
Will in the stormy future sink like lead,
On which unpiloted the nations drive ;
Like one of her own ships, discredited,
That yields to the assault of furious gales.
The scale has turned against her, she declines ;
Chaff in the field her glories of the past,
Dry stubble all in this day's hurricane.
No statesman true on her horizon shows
With power a great occasion to confront,
No hero's daring brow and god-like mien,
Who might those grovelling islanders inspire,
And least of all amid the foremost ranks,
Who lead, or so they claim, the march of mind,
They who preach progress, pah ! they shame the word,
They drag their holy ensign in the mire,
Their creed avowed—to progress true opposed,
Its deadliest foe—utilitarianism ;

The idol at whose gilded shrine they kneel,
And to the facile multitudes present
With oiled persuasion as their living law,
Their faith and God.   The men of science too,
Though in their midst some beaming stars appear,
Celestial souls that shine with steadfast gleam,
Are as a class wrecked on the self-same rock,
Materialism ; for lo, devitalized,
By the slow venom of a false belief,
Which they mislead as pure elixir quaff,
They lose their true relation with the time,
And cannot hence this generation save,
Aroused and moulded by their higher thought,
But, patiently, from brains exhausted weave,
As from his own integuments e'en thus,
The busy spider his light gossamer,
Which, unconcerned, the child's hand sweeps away,
Vain subtleties, baseless though marvellous,
And sophistries, as useful to mankind,
Though in the name of science thrice baptised,
As that frail insect's fragile tenement ;
Greek foolishness, those systems old word-wrought,
Tricked out in modern guise.   Others again,
Bewildered quite, wander in fantasy,

In blind reactions and delusions lost;
Or grope astray in superstition's wood,
Ill-omened and obscure, by spectral ghouls
Haunted of dead beliefs. "Tis pitiful,
With this divided mind, despite her strength,
England more weak and faltering will appear
In European conclave and debate,
E'en than the weakest State. And evermore,
With fatuous skill, the wrong cause she'll embrace,
Ever the wrong path choose, and in that path,
Plant thorns to add to her discomfiture,
Stumbling along with hesitating steps.
All this as in a mirror I behold,
Prefigured in her present; the mystic now,
In whose keen pulse of sharp reality
Commingling meet the future and the past.
Far more hope lies in France, rash headlong France,
Howe'er corrupted by her traitor's reign,
Far more in Russia lies, bold and astute,
Who drinks, barbaric, from primeval wells
A keener instinct of her natural law,
And mandate of the hour. England is doomed,
'Till some convulsion of defeat or shame,
Her nobler nature rouse.

Isis.

Alas, the day !
If fortitude with her unquestioned strength,
And faith and energy could be combined,
And with her good intentions force of will,
What might she not achieve at such a time ?
Establish on a basis her own realm,
By fiercest tempests unassailable,
And from that shore of calm security,
Less favoured nations, to her sun upturned,
Her strong protection then by all desired,
To their salvation lead.

Hyperion.

A fatal flaw
That stubborn " if," for what she might achieve,
She in her folly will not e'en attempt ;
But rather will prefer to wreck her bark
In seeking still to make the flowing stream
Turn backward on its course, the golden sun,
Rise in the glimmering chambers of the west ;
In blindly seeking the fair human tree,
The fostering of her careful hand which claims,

In its thick foliaged growth wide-spread to check ;
Instead of rising on the swelling wave,
In seeking still the vast upheaving main
With man's weak chains to bind.

Aglaia.

If Europe fails
May it not prove that in America,
Whose natal hour so fair with promise shone,
A founded hope for man may still survive ?
While chaos wrecks the Old World's spent domains,
May not sweet peace, more favoured in the West,
In safety dwell and reign ?

Hyperion.

No, surely not.
America long since has forfeited
The grand initiative in freedom's cause
Which in her purer era she assumed,
Like England her once glowing star eclipsed
By sensual mists, a dense and clinging shroud
Of selfishness and greed and unbelief ;
Without sufficient virtue in her blood
Her own unwieldly greatness to sustain.

She has her problems too that must be solved,
Her broad horizon, dark with threatening clouds,
Impending lowers ; but Europe will decide,
Dependent on the crisis of her fate,
Upon her action in the coming years,
For this humanity most critical,
The future of the race ; the destiny
Of every land.   'Tis in these older states,
Where beats with strongest pulse the world's large
    heart,
With discords racked, for renovation ripe,
That must be fought, betwixt the old and new,
The pending conflict not to be delayed ;
There is the battlefield.   And if well fought,
If progress, peace and freedom win the day,
America in that success will share,
In Europe's steps she then will swiftly tread,
And the two continents, regenerate,
In close alliance and strict amity,
Will rule with happy sway the peopled globe ;
The barbarous lands develope and redeem,
And everywhere the reign of law proclaim
And harmony ; but failing here our hopes,
If Europe retrogressive prove too weak

To organise an era more sublime
The race will be at fault ; so we must judge ;
And need not hope in any land or realm,
True progress, true perfection to behold.
No nation now can prosper, none attain,
Or e'en approach the glories of the past,
Unless they all be saved.   The end obscure,
Of this humanity, will be disclosed,
The veil from their dark future thus withdrawn.
The problems solved so sadly in the East,
In painful centuries, with lightning speed,
Will be deciphered in the late-born West,
But with the same result.   In that great realm,
The peace and unity that now prevails,
Harsh violence and discord will dispell,
Dissevered States, in hostile ranks opposed,
And Empires striving for pre-eminence,
And rival kingdoms everywhere appear :
A fitful reign each in their turn enjoy,
Established on the wreck of human hearts,
On war, and poverty, and misery,
And each in turn, fulfilled their pageant dream,
Declining sink, as falls the sapless tree,
In long decay.

Aglaia.

Ah, say no more, enough.
To thee henceforth no more will I repair,
At least when of mankind is our debate.
For comfort in extremity and hope,
For consolation, courage and advice,
Rest well assured. So it has ever proved.
No good in these poor peoples wilt thou grant,
No promise see in their new horoscope,
Which all allow is threatened and obscure.
Prophet of doom, and yet my stedfast faith,
Thy sad prognostications in despite,
And dirge lamentable o'er their defeat,
In this long struggling race I firmly hold,
Maintain in their great future my belief,
Assured at last that o'er these stormy waves,
In triumph to their haven they will ride.

Hyperion.

Prophet of doom ! and yet thou surely know'st,
That in high council in this heavenly sphere,
The Judges of that cause, in state convened,
E'en now have met upon that erring race,

Sentence forthwith to pass ; their destiny
To weigh severe in those remorseless scales
Which Justice in the hour of fate uplifts,
From Mercy then divorced ; if happily
To those discordant states and warring lands
A further respite may accorded be,
Or if their future is beyond repeal,
This problem, this enigma now debate,
The balance trembling still. Thy zeal for man,
Thy hope, anxiety on his behalf,
E'en like thyself to that great being bound,
By deeply rooted and tenacious ties,
I fully share. Despite their wayward course
Uncertain, fitful, reprehensible,
Their faults and darker crimes, this race I love,
And hope most earnestly to see them win,
The meed of this new age, content ;
A glorious future prosperously starred ;
Nay more, the doubtful chance of wavering time,
Uncertain still, deem in their favour turned ;
But who can doubt, confronted sternly thus
By that event, how grave must be on earth,
And dangerous beyond our own belief,
The crisis that prevails.

Isis.

'Tis so indeed,
But for the present, with propitious smile,
Celestial prophecy—O happy thought !
Their course illumes. The conclave has dissolved,
Assembled to decide the fate of man,
And o'er their gathered wisdom hung hope's star.
Not desperate are deemed, though storm-begirt,
The fortunes of the race ; a century,
One cycle still, one more, the most sublime
'Mid all the ages of the pregnant past,
For further trial and endeavour new,
Is granted them, O, brief, momentous years,
Epoch of fate whose course for endless time
Their future will establish or defeat,
In which our efforts we must all augment
On their behalf, and in their doubtful cause,
How urgent that extreme necessity,
Their very life dependent on our care
And toil.

Hyperion.

A century—ten centuries,
Their fate will be declared in half the time.

Isis.

So I believe, nor shall that urgent speed,
If with success the century is crowned,
Deplore ; and that end to promote,
With watchful zeal our part must be performed,
And ardent hope.   At once at their command,
Undaunted, our resources let us place,
No effort, no expedient leave untried,
Their ship in safety o'er these stormy seas,
Perplexed 'mid hidden reefs and dangerous shoals,
Or swept before the gale, to guide at last
To calmer tides.   Amid the shocks of war,
'Mid tumults and transitions dangerous,
Some leader preappointed may arise,
Of tempered spirit, wise and resolute,
Fitted indeed, 'tis not too much to hope,
The claims of this new age to apprehend ;
An instrument divine, whose subtle mind,
Of occult influence susceptible,
We fearlessly can act upon and sway,
And such a one, who in an earlier time,
Must on a lower range perforce have paused,
More limited his service, aim, survey,

In this full present with its broader scope,
Smiting with daring hand the tocsin clear
Whose peal o'er all the nations shall resound,
Uplifting for the welfare of mankind,
That sacred cause supreme, his cheering voice,
May save the world.

Mazzini.

Why have they left me free, mine enemies?
Though fearless I have walked inviting death.
Have none been found, 'mid those who struck down
    Rome
That sacrilege achieved, to strike my breast?
The Captain clings to his abandoned ship,
Goes down with it, deep in the swirling main,
Nor his heroic band does he survive
Who leads to death a hope forlorn: and I,
Shall I alone shame and defeat survive?
One lovely morn, but some few months ago,
A quiet villa's tranquil grounds I sought,

To that sweet haunt of floral bloom withdrew,
E'en thus to meditate.   Bright shone the sun,
A thousand twittering birds sang in my path ;
Flowers bloomed ; sweet children played in happy groups;
And my heart swelled with hope like that young day,
For Rome, from her long apathy aroused,
And by my voice, herself at last appeared ;
The Rome that Dante painted I beheld,
That Virgil sang in thunder-pealing verse,
Whose worship and ideal ruled the past ;
My vision too, embodied as it seemed,
Destined through all the ages to endure,
Ay, for all time.   There I matured the plans,
In that clear sunshine, 'mid those smiling scenes,
Whose wreck amid these ruins I deplore,
In gloom, in solitude, in desolation.
O Rome, unhappy, city of my soul,
As Christ of old wept o'er Jerusalem,
And sought that city of his love to save,
And knew his brooding tenderness in vain,
O'er thee I weep, o'er thee make my lament,
Mine own life I have given to quicken thine,
Thy hope have fed and fostered at my breast,
And must I see thee now, lose faith and fall,

In this dark hour betrayed ? Death is release,
To die and thus your cause still serve sublime ;
The Saviour, his Gethsemane endured,
For those who scourged him perished, thus replied,
Victorious, to mockery and scorn ;
Achieving e'en through martyrdom his end,
Sending e'en from the cross, his hope, his faith,
To quicken in all hearts. Shall I alone,
Lingering importunate in this sad world,
Where they have slain the end for which I live,
Be doomed a cup to drink more bitter still ?
With gall and wormwood brimmed of shattered dreams,
And blasted hopes, the cup of life in death ?

(*He continues to walk in gloomy meditation, while
Federico and the spy advance cautiously a few steps.*)

Federico.

This fool has rushed into the lion's den.
'Tis a rare chance. The Cardinal, you say,
Was likewise notified.

Spy.   .

He was, my lord,
When I discerned yon renegade's design,

Beheld him in this barn forsaken pause,
Like some sick lion swooning in his lair,
To you I hastened bringing the glad news,
A messenger despatched, with urgent speed,
To seek the Cardinal; and charged a third
To summon hither straight our trustiest knaves,
To be at hand, obedient to your call,
In case of need.

Federico.

Wary and prompt, well done.
Prudent at once and bold you prove yourself.
A faithful servant; keep so to the end,
And name your own reward.   Great news indeed :
In such a case to hesitate, content
Upon to-morrow's promise to await,
When bold and resolute leaps forth to-day,
Armed and equipped that service to forestall,
Would seem a tempting of kind Providence ;
Who finding a first boon rejected thus,
All favour might withdraw ; kindness too great
Full oft a snare conceals, is dangerous.
And yet to-morrow's plan was well devised,
Secret and close, and now in every point

Agreed upon.   When will my uncle come?
His will is law, but if elsewhere detained,
Or should he fail his summons to receive,
This enterprize, methinks, I'll venture on,
Presuming in so far on his advice.
For now our victim at the altar stands,
Entrapped, we hold him in our very hand,
And insecure, howe'er it seem to smile,
The future is approved ; for every day,
Each hour at such a time breeds chances new,
Mazzini may escape, suspicious grown,
Be spirited from Rome an hour too soon,
His friends surround him, eager and alert,
From his own headstrong folly to defend ;
Safe as it seems, to-morrow's plan may fail,
And lost, this opportunity unique
Ne'er be regained.   Then I myself forthwith,
The full responsibility will take,
And risk, if such there be, of seizing it.
Shall I the bird ensnared emancipate,
In hopes to wing it in to-morrow's flight ?
A fool might so decide, and lose his pains.
No, 'tis resolved.

Spy.

Your orders, pray, my lord?
The time is passing, and delay a loss.
For now the moon is rising, broad and full,
And will e'erlong this favourable gloom
And twilight dissipate.

Federico.

Be ready all.
The Cardinal may yet arrive in time,
But if he fails, I in his name will act.
Your villains are instructed and well armed,
They know their task?

Spy.

O, perfectly, my lord.
Have no fear on that score, these one and all
Are men of mark, of virtue guaranteed,
Well tried in many a secret enterprise.

Federico.

Our prisoner once too often dares his fate,
He dreams of Rome, in no haste to depart.
Observe him well, but 'till I give the sign,

Hold well your knaves in hand. How still it is;
The ruin is deserted at our need,
No stragglers are abroad ?

Spy

A few, my lord,
Some strangers still are lingering on the walls,
But even now descend.

Federico.

Wait till they go.
When all is safe and silent bring me word,
And when I draw my sword forthwith—despatch.
  (*They step back and are concealed beneath the walls.*)

Mazzini.

Another day will dawn, but not for me.
The sun will rise, but my true sun has set.
No sun henceforth will greet me from these skies,
My feet will tread henceforth on foreign soil,
But one day more, and I shall wander forth,
An exile and an outcast, homeless, lost.
I feel that outer darkness dim and cold,
Gathering e'en now and settling on my soul,

Yet this I would not heed had my work lived,
But that too falls—here my brief triumph shone,
And here it pales ; an instant, phœnix-like,
From sorrow and defeat my life's long aim
As from a blazing pyre rejoicing rose,
And upward soared heaven-high on mighty wing ;
Then stricken by the arrow, reeling fell,
And all is o'er.   How could'st thou fail me, Rome ?
Thou new Republic 'mid the nations blest,
Created by thy people and sustained,
With such bright promise in thy rising star,
Of peace and benefaction to the world,
Thy faith, thy truth, the pledge to Italy
Of her new life, her union, liberty ;
Who now shall sink in dim, chaotic strife,
Her fair, dismembered provinces the prey
Of foreign despots, battling o'er their prize,
Those vampires throned, who drink their victims' veins,
And gather vulture-like, when agonised
In torments they expire ; how could'st thou Rome,
Thy country's trust, and thine own destiny
Thus bitterly deny ?   Could treachery
With Judas' kiss, so grand a hope betray ?
Is evil in this wretched world so strong,

And good so weak ?—still in this age so weak ?
Truth, faith, devotion, these, all these a lie,
The mock, the jeer of guile and crowned deceit ?
Thou vast and melancholy monument,
Which in thy splendour marked the pageant pomp,
And witnessed the decline of ancient Rome,
Ye giant walls that in your wide embrace
Have held how oft barbaric multitudes,
With hot hearts panting for the flow of blood
That cried to heaven, till it brought vengeance down,
And swept away the reign of violence,
The Empire of the world judged and condemned,
Wreck of the past, dismantled yet sublime,
Lone relic of a kingdom now no more,
A star more beautiful than e'er illumed
That fallen State, this fatal day has quenched :
A grander Rome than that which reared this pile,
Is now o'erthrown—founded on liberty,
Which promised to the nations of the earth
Deliverance, o'er all the peoples stretched
The flag of love.   Ye solitary walls,
Why reigneth in your midst this holy calm,
This twilight pause and hushed tranquillity ?
Lo ! here should jackals howl and night birds shriek,

And wandering ghosts rise gibbering from their graves ;
For Italy resurgent is betrayed,
And Rome again has fallen.

　　　　(*He continues to walk and meditate.*)

Spy.

　　　Now, my good lord,
'Tis time, the Coliseum is our own,
'Tis silent and deserted as the grave,
The stragglers have departed one and all,
The outlaw bides alone in the dim gloom,
No bird entangled in the fowler's net
More safe and sure.

Federico.

　　　As silent as the grave.
Fit threshold, O Mazzini, of the tomb
Which yawns e'en now to swallow thee alive,
The lonely cell, where doomed to slow decay,
Like some unburied carcase thou shalt rot,
A spectre, ghost, the shadow of thyself,
Forgotten, lost, unknown ; 'till e'en thy name,
Thy memory, so cherished now and dear,
From fickle Italy's ungrateful heart,
Time shall erase—ill fortune well deserved.
The Cardinal comes not, has lost the hour,

It matters not, this deed, this chance be mine.
How stand your men ?

Spy.

Ready at my command.

Federico (handling his sword.)

Bid them prepare.   Ay, 'tis the fitting hour.
Stand firm, and when I draw this sword, rush forth,
Silent and swift—and mark ! no blunder—mark !
Remember well no blood is to be shed ;
We want no murder reddening on our hands,
The hero slain transforming to a saint,
A victim dangerous e'en in the tomb
When roused on his behalf the people's wrath,
Mazzini disappears, and there an end ;
You know his doom ?

Spy.

His Eminence, my Lord,
Appointed me himself, with his own voice,
This blow to strike ; all the details I know ;
Pray give the sign.
(*As Federico is about to draw his sword, Vittoria, fol-
lowed by a servant, comes from beneath the walls near
the arch where he is concealed.*)

Federico.

Hold, malediction, hold !
By all the Saints the Calendar can boast,
And all the devils who howl in Pluto's realm,
What spectre have we here ?   Why, who is this ?
Great heavens it is no ghost—'tis she herself.
Vittoria here—the Princess here alone !
A rendez-vous, and with this rebel chief—
O, Cardinal, your keen brain is at fault,
Your instinct fails, or this catastrophe,
This infamy would ne'er have been achieved.
Stand close, stir not, move not, upon your lives,
Be firm, and ready to obey my call.
(*Vittoria motions to her servant to remain beneath the
    walls, and advances to Mazzini, led by Hesperus
    unseen.*)

Vittoria.

Hear me, our noble chief, Mazzini, hear !
Some few weeks since—ah, hapless weeks for Rome,
When in our council chamber, your true place,
Foremost you sat, in highest state enthroned,
More royal than a king, the loved Triumvir—

Ah, woe the day that thence has banished you,
For Rome, for Italy, how deep a wound—
Free access to the peoples you ordained ;
And, fearless, trusting in that mild decree,
Women and men your presence sought unblamed ;
Ay ! the poor beggar trembling and in tears,
And children seraph-browed ; all eager came,
With some memorial of that sacred hour,
When firmly stood the people's government,
By brave Mazzini ruled, their stedfast friend,
And Rome was free, their sad and darkened lives
To cheer and bless ; and all—to you the praise—
With hearts well satisfied, their dream fulfilled,
Forth from your presence went.   So day by day,
But in that festive time I stood aloof,
For still I feared your toil to interrupt,
Nor dared on your too heavy burden cast
The added weight of my poor moment's joy,
A selfish claim.   And if unsummoned now,
On your seclusion more sublime of grief,
Your majesty of woe, I dare intrude,
'Tis not without grave cause.   Then pardon me,
And though unclaimed before, not undesired,
Your blessing now accord.

> (*Vittoria kneels and kisses Mazzini's hand.*)

Mazzini (bewildered.)

What gentle voice,
My reverie, too mournful, thus dispels ?
A moment since in sombre night I stood,
Alone amid the ruins of the past,
Mourning, as in a dream, my ruined hopes.
In twilight gloom the Coliseum stretched,
A dim and vacant solitude, immense ;
But as the rising moon her golden disc
Lifts o'er the Eastern wall, illumining
That vague and tremulous obscurity,
All things with splendour strange transfiguring,
A woman's form appears ; and one indeed,
Touched and enhaloed by that mystic gleam,
That fancy might declare, well-justified,
Of more than human grace and loveliness ;
And o'er a silver pathway to my side
With gracious benediction gently glides.
An angel thus, methinks, should minister
To souls in pain.

Vittoria.

Ah no, too kind a thought ;
Could you but read my sad and troubled heart,

You would not deem me thus of blest estate,
But that from heaven some holy seraph sped
To guide my steps, so fearlessly I walked,
At this unwonted hour through these loud streets,
Distracted still and wild with wars' alarms,
With heart so calm and high, straight to my goal,
Ah, that indeed, soothed by the fancy sweet,
I almost thought.   'Twas but a foolish dream,
And yet it gave me strength.

Hesperus (*aside*).

         Alas sweet friends,
With heart that beat so lately one with yours,
And still so prescient of your every thought,
More truly reading you than when on earth,
How strange and sad the severing gulf appears
Dividing us.   With wisdom from on high,
Why may I not your troubled minds imbue ?
Your own pure intuitions bid you trust ?
The yearning faith, the holy aspirations,
Which darkened by your dim and fleshly veil,
E'en when inspired thereby, guided and cheered,
Mere visions you pronounce and idle dreams ?
And yet of your own life which are indeed,

Itself a passing dream, and O, how sad,
Thereof deprived, how vague and meaningless,
These only truth and fact.

Mazzini.

All legends teach
All early lore, and songs of every land,
That unassailed the virgin young and pure,
Protected in her weakness by a charm,
Through dangers which the stoutest heart might quell,
E'en thus serene may walk ; a lovely myth
Which veils a truth profound.　But frankly speak,
Your purpose state, petition and your name.
Yet stay.　Where have I seen your face ?　'Tis true,
My memory serves me well ; a mirror 'ti
That keeps each image once thereon impressed.
I know you, recognize, fair Roman girl,
With your unenvied, rich inheritance,
The blood that courses in your purer veins,
The weight upon you of a sad descent,
And Rome, whom your young life so well has served,
Although with her chief enemies allied,
A race that with just cause she fears and dreads,
Knows you and loves.　Our labours for the state,

By your sweet smile, 'tis true, were ne'er illumed,
Yet voices have not lacked to sound your praise,
Your name, long since familiar, oft I've heard,
And ever with a benediction linked,
That told me what you were ; a heart of gold,
A presence mild of patient tenderness,
Of zeal that faltered not, courage and hope ;
A calm beneficence that went abroad
To heal the sick, to comfort those who mourn,
And from their depths of misery uplift.
I heard and marvelled, for I know your race,
But when I saw yourself my wonder ceased,
For on your brow is written love and faith,
There resignation breathes and fortitude ;
In you I saw one of the noble souls
In woman's form, who held in their strong arms,
And fed upon their breast, imperial Rome
In her grand day, and who no less sublime,
In this our later age, will now, e'en thus,
The fallen state help to regenerate.
Daughter of Italy in her sick throes
What seek'st thou here of me her prostrate chief?

Vittoria.

To plead with you, for your own welfare plead ;

Your safety to ensure, this, this I seek.
I come to warn you of a fatal plot,
Which threatens more than life—your liberty.
O, wherefore have you lingered thus in Rome,
Where every step of yours, as well you know
Treads on a grave? where every breath may prove
The draught of death?

Mazzini.

   Why do I stay in Rome?
Go ask the mother why she kneels and weeps
Beside the cradle where her first born lies
Inanimate; the lover why he clasps,
Bereaved, the clay-cold hand of his new bride?
Why do I linger here? Why stay in Rome?
Rome was my child, my bride, and she is dead,
Dead, yet I cannot tear myself away,
My life, the past, the future, all are here.
My heart strings gather round this sacred land.
I keep my lonely vigil by her corse
Praying e'en here to fall.

Vittoria.

   O, say not so.
Belie not thus your own great work and faith,

Rome is not dead, though now prostrate she lies.
Betrayed she fell, not through her weakness lost,
And soon, the chains new forged that bind her down
In all her greatness rising she will break,
And the bright promise of this darkened dawn,
Whose sun, Mazzini, rose at thy command,
And ne'er will set, howe'er at times o'ercast,
With hope new crowned, in triumph will fulfil,
Your hope in her fulfil. Our sacred Rome,
The city of the past and of our love,
She could not die.

Mazzini.

Young voice of deathless hope,
Sweet as the silver tongue of youth should be
And bold, art thou so prompt to prophecy ?
But tell me this, Vittoria Piombini,
How have you learned, child of your ancestors,
The enemies of freedom and of Rome,
To love your country and to comprehend,
The sympathies profound which vindicate,
Our fallen cause.

Vittoria.

How learned to love my Rome ?

Do I not breathe the air of Italy?
See bending o'er me an Italian sky?
How learned to sympathise with those who weep?
Have I not wept, ah God, what bitter tears?
And how to comprehend the holy cause
To which my soul is pledged, of liberty?
Do I not wear the fetters of a slave?
Why love my Rome?   'Tis in the air, that love.
My servant whom the Cardinal employs
To spy upon my actions and betray,
Comes stealing to my bosom to narrate,
In strains inspired of untaught poesy,
With liquid eyes that flash pure eloquence,
The people's wrongs—a sybil of her faith;
The calm-browed sculptor, in ideal stone,
This fading human form who recreates,
The painter, stern and cold, so to the world,
Who sees upon his canvas glow my face,
The flower which blooms immortal 'neath his skill,
Enchant the hours, when to my ear they speak,
With high discourse, and on the self same theme.
The beggar in the street, who clasps my knees,
Tells the same tale.   Have our young poets sung,
And heroes died, for me alone in vain?

My kindred hate, 'tis true, the people's cause,
And me oppress for loving it so well,
My freedom they would chain, e'en my thoughts bind,
Yet dare they not the holy tasks forbid,
By their own church enjoined, of charity.
And have I freely walked amid the poor,
Our bleeding patriots on this breast sustained,
Brought mangled back from each new, piteous strife
Which hapless Rome has dared ; seen those brave souls
Sail grandly forth from the sweet shore of life,
Where clung and clustered all their well known joys,
With hearts strong in their faith, and haggard eyes
Sublime with hope ;—O, have I seen all this,
Nor learned to comprehend the sympathies
That thrill all Italy and all the world ?
Your words, Mazzini, yours, the living spark,
That woke our country while she slumbered still,
And bade her live, flashing from mind to mind,
Can you believe, O you who uttered them,
That they have failed in my heart to bear fruit ?
The prisoner in his cell those messages
Of holy truth, despite his bars, have reached,
The lonely exile far away inspired,
And soldier in his camp ; nor have they failed,

To find their way e'en to the palace chamber.
How have I learned, you ask, the love of Rome?
Rather, instead, should I of you demand,
How you could doubt that love? and doubt the cause
To which you first gave life.

Mazzini.

Brave words and true.
Ay, true, my child.   Rome as you say, will live,
The Eternal city will not, cannot die,
And from this fall untimely will arise
More powerful than of old.   Your faith is mine.
Your prophecy, my hope, my thought confirm,
Howe'er dim mists, wrenched from the soul's despair,
As whirling snow-drifts in the frozen north
Shroud with unnatural gloom the heavenly vault,
A moment may have dimmed my clearer gaze.
Our Italy, united, strong, and free,
Her true place 'mid the nations will assume,
A queen again, in progress, peace, and art,
With her chief jewel blazing on her breast,
Her mystic sign of power.   All this will be,
Though not perchance in my day nor in yours,
I will not say—the future is obscure;

Yet it will be—and when, leave that to God.
The future will redeem Italia's past.
But yet the Rome we mourn, she will not live,
The Rome of this grand hour, so goddess-like,
From centuries of shame who glorious sprang,
And stood regenerate in her young pride,
The watchword of the future uttering,
The standard high uplifted in her hand,
Of union, freedom, universal peace,
That Rome is dead, defeated, lost and dead,
And she alone was mine. Nay, speak not yet,
Hear me; that words of such deep bitterness,
Though strong within, could cross these close-locked
    lips,
To silence sealed by grief, I did not know;
But you have found me, maiden, and surprised
In my dark hour, when all my stars were quenched,
And sank my soul in the bewildering sea
Of hopeless misery. Grieve not thereat,
For dovelike you have come with olive branch,
To me as welcome as the white-winged bird
To weary wanderers weltering on the wave,
As David's harp brought peace to Saul, your voice
Has lifted the black shadow from my soul,

H

Shows me again the new day's dawn.   No more;
You came you say to tell me of a plot,
Danger I fear not, have invited it,
Have hoped and prayed that on my vanquished head
The bolt suspended in this hour might fall,
But hitherto, as guarded by a spell,
Amid victorious foes unharmed I walk,
No hand has yet been raised to strike me down.
And now that cloud, like death itself, has passed,
And to my breast I clasp defeated life,
For many hopes and lives hang still on mine,
And much may yet be wrought, though in the dark,
Wrought by the exile in cold banishment,
The outlaw and conspirator—my name ;
Nor will I give the foes of bleeding Rome,
Too fortunate, the triumph they now seek,
Of striking once again her prostrate form
Athwart my heart, her bulwark and her shield ;
The secret that oppresses you is mine,
At once disclose it then.

Vittoria.

My name you know,
And family—these all too well alas !

As he his victim smites with secret blow,
And subtly sways the councils of the state,
Seeking to veil not boast his power, e'en thus,
The Cardinal, my uncle, rules our house ;
Sustained in all he does, in all upheld,
By the young prince, his nephew well beloved,
My cousin Federico, to him a son.
For as you know, orphaned I stand, alone,
And they who love me have no power to save ;
So these two tyrants sway my darkened life,
Who are, as all Rome knows, your enemies.

Mazzini.

Poor dove, a cruel fate to nest thee thus,
Within the haughty eyrie, stern and cold,
Of birds of prey.

Vittoria.

More cruel than you deem,
For on my head a title casts its curse,
And this small hand clasps an inheritance,
And therefore must be war, between us, war.
For he, the Cardinal, subtle and bold,
And by his own dark deeds impoverished,

Would on our stronger branch his fortunes build,
And sees in me, essential to his aims,
A prize which must at every cost be grasped,
And by my marriage with his tool secured,
And Federico with his loathsome love
Pursues me night and day, and both unite
By force or fraud to that unhallowed rite,
A union I abhor, to bind me down ;
But rather than consent, a convent's walls
From all delights of life shall shut me out,
Or, better still, a dagger at my heart
End all, and cut the coil with one sharp blow.

Federico (aside).

You Cocatrice ! most base of womankind,
Trust me, but I will make you pay for this
With torments exquisite, and tears of blood.
O Christ—my loathsome love !

Hesperus (aside).

Traitor beware !
For dust will choke your own polluted throat,
And paralyzed will fall your withered arm,
Or ere that threat you execute.

Federico (aside).

Who spoke ?
Methought I heard a voice upon the air ?

Mazzini.

The Cardinal 'tis then, and the young prince,
His heir and nephew, these your nearest kin,
Who have been plotting thus for my defeat ?

Vittoria.

With bitter grief and shame the truth I own,
Last night, a weary age it seems since then,
I sat alone, oppressed by mournful thoughts,
But tenderly the warm air wooed me forth,
And in our garden grounds, secluded, hushed,
A Paradise of rich and tropic bloom,
I wandered 'neath the stars ; and then I wept,
In pity of mine own so helpless state,
And laid my head upon a bank of flowers,
And sleep surprised me there.   From that deep dream,
I woke with sudden start to hear alarmed
The well-known voices of the Cardinal
And Federico : they sat within a bower,

Close at my hand, and those first words I heard,
Breathed imprecations on your honoured name,
And utterly your ruin to achieve,
Disclosed a cruel plot.   Tell me, nay speak,
Have you agreed, that adder in your path,
The Duke Celani, him, your seeming friend,
To meet to-morrow morn—O fatal day !
And has he sworn a secret to disclose,
To Rome of utmost urgent consequence,
Which may perchance win back her freedom lost ?

Mazzini.

'Tis true, and this alone detained me here.
For other friends have urged my speedy flight,
Till yielding at the last to their sad prayers,
My word erewhile reluctantly I gave,
Hence to depart.   Our plans are all arranged,
The means secured, place, hour, agreed upon ;
One day alone was granted of reprieve,
In which, though faithless of his promised aid,
With young Celani I proposed to treat,
And then beheld confronting me my doom ;
A second morn but blank with banishment.
Hither I came in melancholy hour,

To Rome and to the unaccomplished past,
To breathe forth my farewell.

Vittoria.

    A long farewell !
And not to Rome alone, to liberty :
That second morn, though you had still survived,
For you, O chief of Rome, could ne'er have dawned,
No day again have blest your yearning gaze :
A felon heart, a traitor is Celani,   •
A tool, the Cardinal's mere instrument,
Selected to ensure your fall.   A friend !—
Cross but that threshold false and you are lost,
Beyond reprieve irrevocably doomed ;
E'en there is waiting you, implacable,
The execution of their fell decree,
Too horrible to be believed ; not death,
Oh ! no, they would not be so merciful ;
To rot within a dungeon's loathsome walls,
The deepest cell St. Angelo contains,
There linger out an agonized existence,
A life in death of slow, obscure decay,
Lost to your friends, to Italy, the world,
This was the sentence on your head pronounced,

This, this the plot I heard last night disclosed.
E'en thus your noble deeds which they name crimes,
Have they resolved that you should expiate,
And still that fatal meeting they await,
All things arranged, each point, each circumstance,
In false Celani's presence, with his aid,
To seize you and entomb.

Federico (aside).

'   O, viper-tongue.
False traitor to your family and house,
A serpent venomous in woman's form.

Hesperus (aside).

So angels do appear in eyes of devils.

Federico.

Again that whisper ominous—how strange.
No words, and yet a sense of mocking words,
As if mine own soul spoke and threatened me.
A sudden chill runs curdling through my veins,
Freezing my blood ; a sign, so children say,
That on the turf destined to be your grave,
Unconsciously, some idle wanderer treads.
A curse upon these Coliseum walls,

Sepulchral, grim—in this white moonlight's flood
How ghastly, how unnatural they appear—
On them, and every soul that they contain.

Mazzini.

I can believe it, for I know them well.
But I will foil them yet with weapons sure,
More certain than their own though honourable,
And with a word, bid on their head rebound
The dastard blow.   Ay, that had been a fate
More cruel than the exile's lot obscure ;
And haply the unfathomable gloom,
Like death itself, the suffocating pall
Which on my soul so darkly has been cast,
Was but the shadow of their baneful thought,
The presence of that lurking destiny.
But let them know that this my darkened life
For some more noble end has been preserved,
Than e'er to moulder in a noisome cell
At their decree.   An end which they shall feel
Shaking the deep foundations of the State,
And thanks to thee, thou fair patrician flower,
High-hearted maid, with courage so sublime,
By thine own faith and innocence sustained,
Who ventured forth, by danger unappalled,

And fearing not to sunder kindred ties,
An exile's life to save.

Vittoria.

And should I then,
To whom alone the truth had been disclosed,
The bitter truth of that unnatural scheme,
Have seen you sink unaided in their toils?
The holy task I could not thrust aside,
Entrusted me by heaven, of saving you;
My privilege henceforth and only hope;
But in my weakness, trembling and alone,
What fears, what doubts, what torments I endured:
The night passed slowly, for I slept no more,
And when at last the lagging day appeared,
An English sculptor, who reveres your name,
With whom I knew my secret would be safe,
And to whose watchful care, a loyal heart—
Your life, methought, I fearlessly might trust,
I sent in haste to seek. 'Twas all in vain,
Rome he had left, and with no word or sign.
Then with my servant I went forth alone,
Resolved to see you, I myself, and warn,
Or never more to my dark home return,

A roof of treachery on which will rest
The curse of heaven.   All know where you abide,
The great Triumvir's humble home all know.
I sought you there but all was desolate,
Again a useless quest.   A church stands near,
Where patiently I took my stand and there
Awaited your return.   What sick suspense !
The long day darkened down into the night,
And as the weary hours dragged slowly by,
My heavy heart sank failing in my breast ;
More sad I grew, still haunted by the thought,
That I should find the dreadful deed achieved,
Which I in vain had come forth to prevent,
Or that some other blow had struck you down ;
That hapless Rome, robbed of her last defence,
Would ne'er again your noble face behold :
And now in utter woe and misery
I lifted up my soul for help divine,
But silent in the blue vault shone the stars,
No voice replied.   A beggar then passed by,
An old and withered man with keen, black eyes,
Who looked at me askance with glittering smile,
And asked : " What seek you, gracious lady, here ?"
" I seek Mazzini the people's friend," I said.

" A ruin he, and wanders mid the ruins !"
So muttered he, and turning strangely laughed.
But now what heavenly power uplifted me,
What soft breath touched my brow, this I know not,
And ne'er shall know ; but ah ! my heart was flame ;
At once I rose with every doubt appeased,
And steadfast, calm and bold, straight to my goal,
With no delay, no pause, or question asked,
As though a path of light before me stretched,
With steps that faltered not, I hurried on,
As in a dream ; and paused not, nor drew breath
Till here I stood.

Mazzini.

        'Tis strange, ay, passing strange !
But we who live in action may not pause
Such marvels supersensuous to scan,
Save that we note the moment, whose swift flight,
A little draws aside the golden gate
Through which those heavenly intimations stream.
For me I go the future to confront,
And with a heavy heart, on which the thought
Of your sad fate an added burden casts,
For most perplexed I find your gracious morn,
Beset with perils imminent and grave,

And yet 'twould seem a sacrilege to doubt
That one like you, so beautiful and good,
Must claim from watchful Providence a care
Which smiles serene at our poor human fears ;
A heavenly guide, who o'er a path of light,
Your pure and guarded steps will ever lead,
E'en as to-night.   Trust therefore to that thought,
And talk no more in grief of convent walls,
No refuge for a spirit strong like yours,
Nor soothe your fancy with the thought of death,
In life not death awaits you your life's crown.
Trust your own steadfast will, a firm support,
And heavenly grace.   And of one thing be sure.
Though treading as I do a path of gloom,
With evermore a drawn sword o'er my head,
I, least of all, the privilege may claim,
And joy, as it would be, of your defence,
I will not lose you from my sight, or thought,
But from the depths of exile will find means
To greet you oft, and of our plans inform,
And patriotic schemes.   To you I owe
Redemption from a darker doom than death,
And if my life, your gift to-night, serves Rome,
Or Italy, that service will be yours ;

In you an instrument I recognise
By heaven ordained our sacred cause to aid.
Now let us go; to your own home at least,
So far to-night, your young steps I may guard,
And then farewell.

(*As they are turning to leave the Coliseum, Federico ad-
    vances angrily and confronts them.*)

Federico.

A moment, by your leave.
Since this fair Princess of a noble line,
Selects a presence chamber thus apart,
A grand one truly, this majestic ruin,
In which to come by night and hold her court,
This being so, and proved so, as we see,
Perchance she'll not deny some word of grace
E'en to her humble cousin and her slave,
Ere she departs.

Vittoria.

You, Federico, you!

Mazzini (aside.)

The Prince Piombini—ay, 'tis well advise
The first of dramatists, e'en from of old,
A good occasion for a thrilling scene
Dame fortune could not fail to utilize,

Federico, (to Vittoria.)

An uninvited guest, but here I am,
And as your cousin claim an interview,
My right at least.

Mazzini.

Hold, Sir, you are I grant
By sad mischance this lady's relative,
And hence may seem in one sense justified
In urging thus your suit ; but yet forbear ;
For to this lonely ruin desolate
This lady came, through dangers of the night,
In my defence ; to warn me 'gainst yourself ;
A fact which for the present utterly,
For this one hour at least which I may mould,
Your claim annuls. Depart then as you came ;
For 'till her own home shelter her again,
I stand as her protector 'gainst the world,
'Gainst you o'er all though twenty times her cousin,
Speak not, but go your way.

Vittoria.

And wherefore so ?
For you are Rome's defender, Rome's, not mine ;
The champion of all Italy you stand,
Not of a single cause, or single life.

And for my cousin, with his taunts and jeers,
For Federico, him I do not fear.
So low as that indeed I ne'er have sunk,
And if I had; until this very hour,
Though I had trembled on beholding him;
As dreadful as Medusa, though his frown
Had once had power to paralyze my soul,
He would have cured me now by his own act;
For he has followed me, 'tis all too plain,
Has stealthily observed me and pursued,
My secrets to discover and betray.
Ay, he who spends his hours in feasting spies
May well himself at times the same part play,
And truly he has reaped a spy's reward,
In hearing his own praises well proclaimed.
Why should I fear him then? He knows my heart,
More clearly reads it now than e'er before,
Then let him speak.

Mazzini.

If you desire it, well.
But I will here remain, in sight, in call,
Not otherwise.

Federico.

Most surely, great Triumvir.

I should have asked as much, nay, claimed it too.
Your hero gives you leave—Vittoria come.
For you must hear what I would say alone.
(*He leads her some distance off nearer the walls. Maz-*
zini stands in the arena observing them.)

Vittoria (*pausing*).

We are alone, say on.

Federico.

You hypocrite !
False traitor to your house—disloyal girl !
O, I could rend your beauty with these hands
And tear you limb from limb—I could, I could ;
Your beauty, 'tis a mask of guilty shame,
Of brazen insolence and vile deceit.
But no, my passion I must now restrain.
Patience—you think that I have followed you,
Both you assumed it, and Mazzini there,
A spy upon your midnight rendezvous.
'Tis false. Look yonder 'neath yon crumbling wall,
There, in the shadow of that gloomy arch.
What see you there ? seven men armed to the teeth,
My spies, who serve me as one man, my slaves !

I

I learned by chance, no, by a spy's report,
That in this ruin yon foul traitor walked,
And came in haste occasion to surprise,
And execute to-night to-morrow's deed.
You see the men, nay, look, observe them well.
They stand there waiting for a word from me,
A look, a glance, a gesture of this hand,
To lay your hero reeking in his blood,
His course is run.

Vittoria.

Ah God, what words are these?
What do I hear?   No, no, it cannot be.
It is some dreadful dream.

Federico.

No dream, a fact.
I came not armed against the felon's life;
No, bent alone the scheme to carry out
Which you, most dove-like Innocence, betrayed.
But with the time my purpose too has changed.
I would not trust him, knowing what I know,
Within the deepest dungeon ever dug,
With triple walls of brass begirt; not I.
O, he would find his way out, never doubt,

And come with that detèsted brow serene,
Unblanched and fearless to confront us all.
No, he shall die; his dungeon now shall be,
A safe one this at least, the silent grave.
Thus too, I make you feel my just revenge,
Ay, you shall see the wretch you came to warn,
· Struck down by your own hand, slain and by you.
So now prepare.

Vittoria.

What is't that I must do?
Speak, speak, O you have tortured me enough.
What is't you seek?

Federico.

Retract the words you spoke,
Swear by the tears of Christ and bloody sweat
To be my bride, and when and how I choose,
Give me that pledge, or by my living soul,
You know me, and will trust my word at least,
He, on the instant dies.

Vittoria.

Never, so help me God.

Federico.

Take time, the life is hanging on your breath,
Which you so dearly prize—Mazzini's life.
Three minutes, five, I give you to decide;
Nor turn to him, dare that and he is slain;
Nay, hold, a single glance and it is done.
Reflect and speak.

(*Federico stands between Vittoria and Mazzini, and
takes out a watch to note the time.*)

Vittoria.

    Angels of light and peace,
Ye spirits merciful who dwell on high,
And pity in sweet heaven our human woes,
Help me, O help and save.

Hesperus.

    Thy prayer is heard,
Fear not, sweet human heart, and tremble not,
The tempter who contends with thee resist,
Resist him and defy.

Vittoria.

    By that deceit,
That desecration to destroy my soul,

Yield all my future to despair and shame

Hesperus.

Hold not vain counsel with thy troubled mind,
But to thine own unerring instinct trust,
And fearlessly the foe that tempts defy.
Give thou no pledge, no lawless compact form,
Thy freedom in the future which would bind,
And force thee to pursue a shadowed path,
Where thy young soul's white innocence would pale,
Defeating thus by one mistaken act,
That lures thee in the name of sacrifice,
Thy life's appointed aim.

Federico.

One minute gone,
Have you resolved ? Not yet ? Nay, take your time,
Four yet remain.

Vittoria.

O, cruel heart—ruthless !
How pale Mazzini in the moon-light stands,
Of danger all unconscious, calm, serene,
With earnest eyes on me fixed steadfastly,
Like some high angel watching o'er my soul,

There stands, there waits my safety to ensure,
From peril and alarm me to defend,
While o'er his own head hangs the thunderbolt,
In these few counted moments doomed to fall,
To one dread point which dwindle while I speak,
Assailed, cut down by murderous hands unseen,
Stabbed, murdered in my name. Ah, God of heaven,
That must not be. How could I live henceforth,
How from this hour walk forward into life,
With that pale form stretched bleeding at my feet,
Reproaching me who saw and would not save,
Reproaching me in death, with solemn eyes,
And pallid brow ensanguined 'neath my gaze,
Who feared my paltry life to sacrifice,
My hopes, my dreams, my future to resign,
To save for Italy her martyred chief.

Hesperus.

Trust thou in God, trust in the God of Love
Who marks the stricken sparrow as it falls,
And shields his children all with fostering wing ;
Anchor in the Eternal God thy faith,
And do no evil deed that good may come.
Lo, who art thou Mazzini to defend ?

Are there no higher dread Divinities
The dedicated soul beloved to shield?
Deemst thou in dull forgetfulness they sleep?
Abate thy pride, presumptuous and rash.
Mazzini's life is guarded and secure,
Fear not for him but tremble for thyself;
Fear lest the tempter lead thee now astray,
Persuading thee, by doubt and fear assailed,
The freedom of thy spirit to forswear,
To heaven make thy appeal.

Vittoria.

Who uttered it,
The dread command, the solemn invocation
That seems e'en now to tremble on the air?
The sacred monitor that dwells within,
And with authority one course directs,
In conscience the eternal God revealed,
Is't that which thus commands me and enjoins,
Seeming for my soul's welfare and repose
To supplicate? or can it be indeed,
That by my side, with watchful tenderness,
Descending merciful from highest heaven,
To guide me on my troubled path aright,

With dream-like voice, soft as a zephyr's breath,
Heard only by my spirit, low, intense,
A soothing presence, calm, beneficent,
The hovering wing of Deity, unseen,
Some holy angel bends ; a friend divine,
Who in this hour of fear and anguish seeks
To soothe and strengthen me.   Oh, can it be ?
Could I in the divine assurance trust,
Which from an unknown source, impalpable,
I seem, though how I know not, to receive ?
Could I believe ?

Hesperus.

Thou canst poor child of earth,
Perplexed in thy so dim and darkened path.
Believe, sweet maiden, doubt not but believe.
Thy faith exalts thee and thy doubts betray.
'Tis true that by thy side an angel stands,
That angels tenderly thy course observe,
And bend above thee to protect and guide,
We love thee well and pity thy despair,
O, trust us and obey.

Vittoria.

I hear it still,

That heavenly voice—that inward monitor.
But 'tis in vain, all, utterly in vain !
O, agony too great to be endured.
How dare I in the frantic hope confide,
The wild, despairing hope of heavenly aid,
When on my breath and will suspended hangs
A human life, and that Mazzini's life.
Will Federico yield, that cruel heart ?
No, hate alone is written on his brow ;
I dare not that resolvèd will defy,
And fear no less the voice to disregard,
Which seemed like heaven itself commanding me,
So tender soft and pitiful—so kind,
Sweeter than human speech—O, I am mad !
Bewildered by this sudden blow I rave,
Persuade myself that what I wish to be,
Because I wish it therefore must be true,
That these wild yearnings beating in my brain
Are voices sent from heaven to hold me back
From the abyss yawning upon my path
In which remorselessly I now must plunge.

Federico.

'Three minutes gone—one only now remains,
But one—and then.

Vittoria.

Hold, Federico, hold !
One moment only, one last breath of life.
Ye supplications, mild and pitiful,
Ye murmured prayers, ye whisperings half heard,
That throb around me still with soft reproach,
And which erewhile to my bewildered heart,
Of some bright presence the assurance seemed,
Divine suggestions, warnings, intimations,
The voices sweet of friends beneficent,
Oh cease, let me your unreality
Confess ; or otherwise, if true my dream,
If in this hour some spirit from on high
Has sought, beholding my unhappy need,
Celestial aid and comfort to impart
To one unworthy proved of heavenly grace,
If from my holier hope I now decline,
My human weakness, oh, sweet Saint, forgive,
For all my strength in weakness is dissolved,
Or all my weakness nerved to higher strength,
I know not which, but this, this only know,
That I no longer can contend ! 'Tis o'er.
The destiny that like a threatening cloud,

Has hung impending o'er me from the first,
Is now fulfilled ; this hour decides my fate ;
E'en from the first to misery foredoomed,
My life here ends ere well it has begun,
The struggle ceases ne'er to be renewed ;
Heaven claims from me this awful sacrifice,
Then let me render it without complaint.
I feel the shadow closing over me,
I hear the clanking of my dungeon door,
And quench with mine own hand the lamp within—
So let it be—one sorrow I escape,
No burden on my soul of blood shall rest,
Of other lives for my sake blotted out,
And one high thought shall cheer me on my way,
That my defeat has saved for Italy—
A prize worthy its cost—her noblest son,
And with that life, her freedom, her new hope ;—
Federico hold—-forbear unhappy boy ;
I yield to your demand.

Federico.

    You speak in time ;
If still your foolish purpose you retain,
Of keeping yon vexed spirit on the earth,

With none tò lose ; his sands of life had run.
Three seconds I allowed, so much for grace
And on the point of doom the dial turns.

Vittoria.

You swear at least that he shall go unharmed.

Federico.

My faith I pledged to that in claiming yours.
And I will hold my faith, as you shall do.
Ay, let the outlaw go, I heed him not ;
My mind has other objects now in view.

Vittoria.

Another victim now whom you may strike.

Federico.

That we shall see in time ; now let us hence ;
Mazzini waits your homage to receive,
Bid him farewell, and calmly or beware !—
'Tis your last sight of him, be sure of that,
And he, not I, despite his insolence,
Will be your escort to your home to night ?
But who are these ?

(*A band of young Italian soldiers, who have been in-
stigated by Hesperus to seek for Mazzini, rush in and
surround him.*)

Hesperus (to Federico).

Traitor, the sword of heaven.

(*To Vittoria.*)

Unhappy child, woe, woe, what hast thou done ?

Vittoria (bewildered.)

Ah, me, unhappy, woe, what have I done ?

Federico.

Sold me your liberty and without cause.
Mazzini's angels guard him, mark—behold !—
See that brave band of Italy's young blood
'Gainst whom my secret bravoes must have fled.
Lo, said I not that he would rise unharmed,
E'en from our dungeon, had we buried him.
But you are mine, I hold you to your bond.

SCENE IV.—*The atmosphere of the planet Mira. Grand Convocation of Ethereal Spheres. The Guardian Host of the planet occupies a central position, the other Hosts being grouped about it, so as to form a semicircle.*

Una.

Celestial spirits various of all ranks,
Immortal Hosts of beautiful Immortals,
Fair Majesties of Heaven ; ye lovely groups
Who round me scintillate like throbbing stars,
We need not now declare, to all well-known,
Of this momentous and high festival,
Ordained by mandate of the Soul Eterne,
Which from remotest magnitudes of space,
Has to this constellation summoned forth,
Vast in extent and in resources rich,
This beaming galaxy of heavenly spheres,
The happy cause. To aid and bless we come,
In their young life the gracious Miranites,
A noble race of promise and renown,
Who rule beneficent their native globe,
The planet fair, sweet as a new-blown rose,
Now sheltered by our soft and fostering wing,

And by our smile illumed. Most fortunate
In her late course this radiant orb has proved,
For while her earlier peoples, apathetic,
The mystic word of progress failed to catch,
Long since in dread succession swept away,
As each in turn an incomplete career
Blindly fulfilled, too languid and inert
Their higher destiny to comprehend
The monarch of the renovated globe,
Erewhile by her protecting Host transformed,
Her last created fair Humanity
Treading with front erect her fruitful plains ;
These noble peoples of transcendent strain,
Whose high achievements and immortal deeds
We meet on this great day to celebrate,
Their goal appointed in the march of time,
That glorious goal for which all races strive
But few attain, of love and harmony,
Already in their spring and glowing dawn
Have early won. With every grace adorned,
And loveliness, in full perfection blooms,
The cultured globe protected by their care,
The planet Mira, rich, prolifical,
The ornament of that effulgent star,

A potent sun of primal magnitude,
Who in this teeming system reigns supreme,
The queen confessed of his resplendent train.
Societies and federated states,
In amity and holy peace allied,
An earlier age beheld well organized,
The daring deed and conquest of the past,
While of the present in its fuller scope,
The ruling Spirits, Seers and Potentates,
They who the happy nations now protect,
And guide them in their upward soaring path,
Those pure and lofty minds, with wisdom crowned,
The blissful reign of universal love,
Of freedom and collective harmony,
Destined through all the ages to endure,
Ay 'till the mother orb, fulfilled in time,
The cycles vast of her immense career,
Shall perish and decay, prepare e'en now
In pomp to solemnize. This high event
A far seen landmark loftily upreared,
Through all the ages to commemorate
The dawn triumphant of their era blest,
With heavenly gratulation to approve,
To quicken and arouse the yearning peoples,

And fortify the purpose of their Seers,
For this great cause o'er Mira's glowing breast
These radiant Hosts in splendour congregate ;
'Mid whom our place assume, our part perform.
Uplift ye Choruses, your tuneful strains,
Swelling anew with one more voice of praise
The countless harmonies whose rhythmic waves
All space with throbbing ecstasy o'erflow.
Shed down upon the globe pure effluence shed,
The rain impalpable of heavenly love,
The dew beneficent of heavenly grace,
The benediction of the blissful Hosts.

*In obedience to Una's command the newly arrived Host
assumes its place in the Heavenly Convocation, the
Choruses chaunting divine strains, and shedding an
effiux of heavenly light upon the planet.*

Chorus.

Soul of Nature !   God of all !
Source of every blessing !
First upon thy power we call,
Thine in ours confessing,

K

Let that radiance which is thine,
Through thy spheres in glory shine.

Orb of beauty !   Planet bright !
    O'er which now we hover,
Catch from thy sphere access of light,
    New delights discover ;
Fly with freshly plumèd wings,
On to ever better things.

Bask in novel beams of bliss,
    Blest with heavenly favour ;
Sip thy Sun's parental kiss
    With a sweeter savour ;
Glories of a new-born day
Light thee on thy wonted way.

Noble people, take the meed
    Of a great endeavour,
Higher thoughts and powers, to lead
    Up and up for ever,
Great and ever greater light
Due to those that use aright.

Thrilled with holy fervour feel
   Your regeneration,
And receive as we reveal
   Nobler inspiration ;
In your new propitious clime
Feel your wings and soar sublime.

The Choruses of heavenly effluences continue unintermittingly. Countless groups of angels overlook the scene.

Orion.

How far imagination's ardent flight
Reality, the living fact, transcends.
What kindled brain a scene so marvellous
With fancy all aglow could e'er conceive ?
Or e'er the vision unbeheld, portray ?
Encradled in her sun-thrilled atmosphere,
And glittering 'neath the sheen of these bright heavens,
How perfectly the attributes divine,
And qualities of her celestial sphere,
This planet fair reflects. In nature's face,
Full flushed in sweet excess of glowing bloom,
Each gorgeous hue and shape symmetrical,
A reproduction of ethereal scenes.

Amid the systems numerous and groups
Whose beaming flocks in their bright course we tend,
Few do I now recall of rarer charm,
More fitted noble races to sustain,
And to assume within the planet realm
A place distinct of marked significance,
And lofty rank.

Procyon.

           'Tis so beyond dispute.
This lovely Mira, this fair planet flower
Has to us all afforded a surprise.
Ay, now indeed, in this immortal hour,
The daring of her Host in venturing
The younger globe discordant to redeem
A worthy recompense must find. Observe,
With swift and subtle gleam illumining,
As suddenly they flash through kindled space,
The pure effulgence of this love-lit realm,
Bright troops of Seraphim from all the spheres,
Ardent, with simultaneous movement flash,
And thither speed. In sweet companionship,
Down-swooping eagerly on wings of love,
The planet's lower atmosphere they seek,

And radiant o'er her happy multitudes,
Like some dawn-gilded irridescent mist,
Or golden exhalation of the morn,
Or sunset-cloud, scarce veiled in roseate flame,
Suspended float.   How exquisite a sight;
The beauteous globe quivers and palpitates
As they rain down their lightnings on her breast,
Celestial beams and potent rays of love,
Entwining her with fetters strong and sweet,
With her ethereal star, from whence she draws,
A source exhaustless of pure energy,
Her vital flame.   Could now her peoples blest,
To their full scope of consciousness awake,
Find, one and all, their spirit eye unsealed,
This glorious pageant in the air behold,
As we delighted mark their festival,
The joy and exaltation of the hour
Would be complete.

Hyperion.

That too will be attained.
A race so fair and loftily endowed,
Our highest hope will fail not to fulfil,
Securing of their earlier victories

The golden crown.   Since their last festival,
That rare occasion, high and fortunate,
The reign of law establishing and peace,
Not once in this bright realm, so has it chanced,
Has my full stream of life made pause, and now,
Amazed at their unlooked for growth I stand.
These peoples walk sublime in grace and power,
And fragrant blooms, an Eden of delight,
Their radiant orb.   Now hearkening their discourse,
The consultations of their leading minds,
Almost perfected their collective life
I find, and glancing broadly o'er the globe,
Including in one view kingdoms and states,
In their harmonious and wise governments,
United all like one great family,
Detect no flaw.   Ay, mark my prophecy,
When next in festive state we here assemble,
'Twill be the final act to celebrate ;
The grand transfiguration of the race,
And entrance on transcendent harmony,
To privileges rare admitting them,
Unchecked communion with the Heavenly Hosts,
And Spirits blest.

Isis.

And thou, my Hesperus,
Does this bright pageant in the radiant Spheres
Thy expectation and desire fulfil,
And for thy planet's loss in part console ?

Hesperus.

Ravished with ecstasy I scarce can speak,
These beaming Hosts in their resplendent groups,
With light, with life, with joy o'erflowing space,
These dazzling Galaxies of living Suns,
These throbbing Legions mercilessly bright,
My soul's capacity to apprehend,
To feel and to enjoy well nigh defeat ;
For once before amid these radiant ranks,
Once only I have stood, wondering, awe-struck,
And veiled, as well thou know'st, they then appeared,
For in that fearful hour the lovely earth,
The group in which she whirls and other realms,
Although unconscious of their threatening doom,
Hung agonized e'en on destruction's verge,
And stern and pale in panoply of war,
'Gainst natures forces armed and elements,

With fate confronted pitiless and death,
As angels may we battled then, o'erwrought,
Silent, with baited breath, invincible,
A universe from ruin to redeem,
Those worlds to save—O immemorial strife !
Thus terrible, thus dread, although sublime,
And not as now in splendid state adorned,
Sunlike.   And nature too in pomp unveiled,
In these strange aspects unimagined seen,
In these wide plains of vacancy beheld,
Illimitless ; this constellation vast,
Transcending far in magnitude our own,
And in magnificence ; yon glorious sun,
Like God supreme high blazing o'er our heads,
Essential Deity in state enthroned,
With his attending, regal satellites,
And glancing planet train, so swift, so bright,
Whirling upon their orbits full in view,
These moving landscapes, indescribable,
These congregated and majestic worlds,
My senses daze, bewilder quite my mind,
Astonish me, o'erwhelm ;—and still beyond,
Ah me—beyond, in space, infinitude,
Where'er I gaze new systems I behold,

Innumerous, new groups, new constellations,
For stronger my celestial sight has grown,
And fitted these wide vistas to embrace,
Where'er I gaze abysmal depths profound,
A background of unfathomable gloom,
Thrilled and electrified with those quick fires,
That whirl and glow, that throb and scintillate,
That close around me and allure my soul.
I tremble in these clear, ethereal heights,
Fearing on life, on heaven, my hold to lose,
And sink uncentred through the shuddering voids,
For ever lost in space.

Isis.

It is not strange.
Thou to a stern ordeal art exposed.
These glowing landscapes of the Universe,
These cosmic splendours of the awful sphinx,
In all their dread sublimity unveiled,
In all their vast immensity beheld,
Grandeur and glory inconceivable,
No angel, brightest 'mid the heavenly ranks,
Although his gaze entranced has fed thereon
For æons and for ages numberless,

Unmoved shall contemplate ; ne'er shall behold,
Through all the æons of eternity,
Nor feel his breast with deep emotion stirred.
Then wonder not in thy unwonted youth,
Now first confronted with the awful voids,
The dread infinitudes, no, wonder not
To find thy spirit shattered and o'erwrought,
Thy very soul o'erwhelmed. So it must be,
Until by use and custom fortified,
And sublimated by thy heavenly life,
Thy tempered nature stronger has become
And more serene ; then for the present seek,
Enduring patiently, as best thou canst,
A strange experience beyond thy strength,
From these transcendent sceneries thy mind,
And from the flashing splendours of these Hosts,
Howe'er enticing prove the contemplation,
Quiescent to withdraw. Forget them all,
The whirling groups and the effulgent heavens,
And claiming now thy thought, on yon sweet globe,
The planet fair o'er which we hovering brood,
Thy dazzled and bewildered gaze direct,
There fix, there concentrate thy wandering thoughts,
There seek repose.

Hesperus.

Nay, that is mockery.
For there no less what landscapes marvellous,
What dazzling scenes, what gorgeous spectacles,
Reflecting the bright pageant viewed on high—
Although that thought a sacrilege may seem
And is perchance—we everywhere behold ;
What splendour inconceivable and pomp,
Is then likewise displayed beneath our view.
On that sweet globe so have I turned my thoughts,
There bent, as though imploringly, my gaze ;
Demanding from that lower planet realm,
In nature like my native earth repose,
There seeking rest ; and yet no rest I find,
But cause alone for wonder, new delight,
Astonishment and awe.

Procyon.

And yet methinks,
For one so high o'erwrought in ecstasy,
So dazed and blind and wildered, as thou say'st,
Thy bearing reassuring doth appear,
Which to thy friends encouragement affords,

Who would not wish to see thee in the voids,
Like some wild star shot madly from its sphere,
Extinguished utterly, so young, and lost—
Thy outward aspect this at least serene.

Hesperus.

Ah, now indeed serene I may appear,
For now my self-possession I resume,
Each instant stronger feel and more assured,
New life and vigour flowing through my veins
E'en as I speak ; but trust me, ne'ertheless,
For some uncounted moments terrible,
I call them so because too high and dread,
Or hours, ah me, in heaven time dwelleth not,
For what to me an endless time appeared,
While ye, absorbed, naught noted of my state,
I feared in these immensities to swoon,
All thought, all life, all consciousness o'erwhelmed.

Procyon.

Nay tremble not, take heart. In such a scene,
In this irradiate tempest of delight,
This joyous storm by these bright Hosts evoked,
'Mid lightnings of the spheres and fulgurations,

And yonder lovely globe's festivities,
'Tis true indeed that scarcely shall thy soul
In these wide-glancing fields a refuge find
Or foothold of repose.   Like birds astray,
In some wild tempest caught, electrical,
'Twixt heavy-laden and magnetic clouds
With flaming lightnings charged and thunderbolts,
Contending in a fearful rivalry,
That volleying artillery to exchange,
Tossed to and fro on wild and frightened wing,
Between these sharp extremes of ardent life,
These palpitating and responsive poles,
The world beneath and flashing heavens above,
Entangled and ensnared thy thoughts appear,
Between them hurled, bewildered and amazed,
With oscillation vain ; for when on high,
By splendours unendurable assailed,
Thy spirit faint and fluttering flees below,
But only in that world to be o'erwhelmed,
And to return, dazzled by planet scenes,
To be anew within the upper sky,
Distracted and dismayed.   But courage yet,
Although bewildered thus thy mind now seems,
Ay, for the present, hopelessly distraught,

Fear not; more calm wilt thou e'erwhile become,
And learning thy amazement to restrain,
Will likewise learn these spectacles sublime,
These everwhirling panoramas swift
To face and contemplate with steadfast eye,
And from that contemplation unalarmed,
True pleasure unalloyed wilt thou derive,
Since less o'erwrought by feeling in excess,
And happiness untold.

Isis.

Bear too in mind
The caution that I gave thee, well-advised.
Abstracted from the bright infinitudes,
And vistas scintillant that lure above,
Seek still thy wavering and uncertain thoughts
On yon fair globe solicitous to bend;
Which soon undazzled thou shalt contemplate,
With peaceful satisfaction undisturbed,
And which thy duty calls thee to observe,
Since 'twas alone for that sweet planet's sake,
That these fair Legions, in their grand array,
On outspread pinions wafted of swift love,
Athwart the glancing orb-bespangled voids

Have hither sped ; of every heart and mind
The object now, preoccupation, care,
And which no less from thee attention claims ;
In festive pride and loveliness adorned,
Thy admiration it will well repay,
A beauteous orb, is't not ?

Hesperus.

Ah, more than that.
No words, heaven—sweet, shall ever say how fair.
To me at least who know of planet realms
One globe alone, and that my native earth,
Beyond expression marvellous appears,
Almost incredible, the splendid state
Thereon displayed. Ah me, what aspects grand
Hath nature in that favoured realm assumed,
How sweet the smile of her strange countenance
And nameless charm. Far as the eye can reach,
And that a circling hemisphere includes,
Sweeping with broad survey o'er land and sea,
Vast mountain ranges on pellucid skies
Their outlines strange and grandiose project,

While tranquil vales, embowered in verdure rich,
Unfathomed depths of calm repose reveal.
The forests tower heaven-high with monarch growths,
A foliage far more gorgeous than the earth's,
While streams and oceans, clear as flawless glass,
With waves more buoyant bound and prouder tides
Than heave our mundane seas. Strange creatures too
Most wondrous, unexampled, I behold.
The lower animals, magnificent,
Superb in form and hue and varied type ;
While that chief race who level stands with man,
And hence in chief my love and reverence claims,
So god-like moves in grace and majesty,
And loveliness almost angelical,
That tears bedew mine eyes as, reverential,
The earth's ambassador, for so I feel,
I greet him for mankind. And in his works,
The culture and adornment of the globe,
The realms and kingdoms by his hand evolved,
That subtler nature ultimate named art—
Lo, how his wisdom shines : supreme he reigns,
The seal of his great mind on all things cast
The traces everywhere of his strong hand,
Of patient skill with intellect informed

And long enduring toil.   How rich in hope,
These fruitful fields and golden harvests wave,
What brooding happiness and dove-eyed peace,
In yon sweet Edens of sequestered bloom
Enamoured nest.   With stately fanes adorned,
With gleaming palaces and sculptured shrines,
And great creations of transcendent arts,
With fount and grove and deathless shapes ideal,
How lovely shows the net-work of fair towns,
And cities, domed and spired, imperial,
That gem, like clustering stars, the planet's breast,
What sumptuous wealth in all conspicuous,
What symbols everywhere of knowledge, power,
And what rejoicings in them all, world-wide,
And festive mirth.   From north to south, from east
      to west,
The whole vast globe like one sweet blossom smiles,
One scene of triumph and delight displays,
One glad fête celebrates.

Orion.

      Ay, sweet the song
Which Mira fair, that planet of delight,
Is chaunting high to these ethereal spheres,

L

One voice including voices manifold,
Commingled strains and interblended notes,
Which, as the ocean's solemn monotone,
The babbling speech confused of myriad waves,
Their wistful sighings soft and whisperings,
In its eternal lullaby resumes,
The diapason deep which through all time,
The raptures of the waters celebrates,
With their creator babbling, heart to heart ;—
In one eternal hymn, one swelling chaunt,
One full-toned, universal symphony,
To heaven ascends.

Hesperus.

                    Thou speakest in metaphor ?
Or hast indeed plain fact and truth declared ?
For lo, methinks, the murmurs heard below,
The planet's voices multitudinous,
Of speech, of song, the countless jubilations
Which sweet in separation I detect,
Are thus indeed in one pure hymn resolved,
And heavenward soar as one commingled strain,
A harmony divine.   'Tis surely so,
With subtle waves intense, scarce audible,

Heard more than felt, it beats upon my breast,
That floating hymn, that perfect symphony,
The soul of those dissevered, happy strains,
That to the sensual ear make their appeal,
The song of life that from that grateful race
Ascends on viewless wing to God's high throne ;
The planet too in her transcendent flight
A soaring anthem chaunts, and that as well,
I now begin though faintly to detect ;
Sweet, O how sweet, but yet impersonal,
Delicious, vague, a dream-like, hovering note,
Distinct from that full anthem more assured,
To which in soft accompaniment it sighs—
As to a singer's voice some instrument,
With faint and fitful swell and fall, half-heard—
The song of living souls.   Ah, gentle friends,
Sustain me, for again my spirit droops,
With bliss extreme, with ecstasy o'erwhelmed,
Falters anew ; the echo I have heard,
Now first in these celestial fields have caught,
Of that pure harmony, ineffable,
Of which great souls upon the earth have dreamed,
And in their inner world e'en there have heard,
The Music of the Spheres.

Orion.

Most blessed the hour
Which to the mind that revelation brings,
As yet thy faculties seraphical,
In their essential potency unformed,
Are vague and tremulous.   The time will come,
E'en as a skilled musician, subtly-souled,
At some great symphony or opera,
Who in the work he hears each motive marks,
Each movement traces in its wayward course,
Its gradual, exquisite development,
Each sweeter strain and wingèd phrase enjoys,
And, jarred thereby, each phrase inconsequent,
Discordant, false or weak, these suffers from ;
The value of each note determining
In that enwoven web of melody,
Its place and meaning in that living woof
All tremulous of sound ; thus highly trained,
With full appreciation, sensitive,
As that musician hears or reads his scroll,
And judgment on that work doth then pronounce,
Prepared by his own skill to judge thereof,
Its merit sealing with approval glad,

Or, worthless found, condemning it with pain,
Shalt thou, in thy sublime maturity,
With apprehensive skill and trained delight,
These spheral chaunts and cosmic symphonies,
God-like attend.   For through their varied strains,
The fortunes of the orb that utters them
Will to thy mind be instantly revealed;
Its state, development, condition, phase,
And of each soul that dwells thereon the state;
Each good deed there recorded thou shalt mark,
And each base deed therein revealed deplore,
Each aspiration pure and winged desire
Thine own celestial mind will reillume,
Each base thought sadden thee and cloud thy joy,
The notes and motives of that planet hymn,
That song sidereal.   So beat, so sigh,
With ceaseless waves that ebb and flow forever,
On the dread shore of the Eternal Throne,
The hymns and anthems of the Universe.
And there, the central Spirit uncreate,
Ineffable, the ever-living God,
Hearkens of all created souls the voice,
Their prayer attends, their destiny evolves,
With all communion holds.

Hesperus.

                    High mystery,
The truth whereof e'en now I apprehend,
E'en now in part exerting that great gift.
O, wondrous hour of all revealing bliss,
O, happy globe which reads me this sweet lore,
Delightful scenes that fascinate and charm.
Ah me, how sad and pale my planet shows,
Paltry and poor, viewed in comparison
With this resplendent star.   And yet sweet friends,
One thought persistently my spirit haunts,
In which my yearned-for rest at last I find,
The refuge of my dove-winged, weary soul,
My Ararat in these o'erflowing joys,
Ay, there at last repose.   Despite its pomp,
Its splendour undeniable and charm,
As I erewhile of heaven itself pronounced,
So of this globe I say : " 'Tis like the earth ;"
And like mankind this proud humanity
Of regal strain.   Surely between the two
A close resemblance palpable I note,
Most evident, and not to be o'erlooked,
These god-like peoples of majestic mien,

More tall in stature, fairer, more divine
Than that inferior race ; more lovely far
Than in their present low estate they stand,
Or, yearning up through fructifying time,
Can hope in endless æons to become,
Are yet my kindred, my transfigured friends,
In form, expression, countenance well-known ;
And so too with the globe, these glowing scenes,
These mounts, these streams, these undulating plains,
Though outlined in proportions vast, do still
In her most radiant aspects when beheld,
Her seasons mild, and in her loveliest lands,
Mine own sweet earth recall.

Isis.

Ah, Hesperus,
When longer thou hast dwelt in these fair realms,
When from sweet nature's face in many worlds,
And many glowing systems thy young hand
Has drawn aside with reverence the veil,
Thou wilt not marvel thus, more calm thy mind,
And deeply with celestial lore imbued,
Where'er, athwart the star-bespangled voids,
Thy gaze is turned, with ever new delight,

Similitude to find.   For unity,
This still is sacred nature's central law,
Whereof the reflex principle is change,
Few constant types, clothed in variety
She everywhere presents.   All planet globes,
Throughout the constellated Universe,
In their essential elements and forms,
Their fundamental structure and design,
All destined living creatures to sustain,
And to the same great laws obedient,
Of motion, birth, vicissitude, decay,
Howe'er, in outward aspects various,
And in their phases of development,
One thought reflect.   Yet truly hast thou read
In the great volume of the mystic sphinx,
The glowing page which now thy thought arrests.
The marked relationship, discernible,
In planets all, that swift community,
The family of congregated globes,
'Twixt Mira and the earth unusual shows,
Here most significant.   Seek as thou wilt,
'Mid systems fair and constellations rich,
That strew with sands of stars the fields of space,
Yet scarce a second orb shalt thou behold,

So like the earth as this delightful star
That now thy gaze enchants.   Ay, sister realms
They float responsive on their whirling course,
And, thus allied, one pathway should pursue,
One destiny fulfil.

Hyperion.

'Tis much to claim.
Twelve times in size this orb magnificent
And beautiful, our planet doth exceed,
And in fertility, in wealth and pomp,
All regal and transcendent attributes,
By living satellites attended mild,
And wearing at each pole a splendid crown,
Whose beams auroral and electrical,
Her atmosphere thrill and invigorate,
A thousand fold perchance ; incalculable,
Beyond comparison, in all these points,
Her higher state.   In soil and temperature,
In zones and climes and times and periods,
Their similarity none will dispute,
But while the shadowed earth thus doubtful whirls,
Uncertain in her course and undeveloped,
We scarcely should pronounce them " sister orbs ;"

Or venture to assert that thus allied,
They of necessity one path will tread,
One destiny illustrious achieve ;
Our petty grub, obscure and retrogressive,
A glowworm at the best whose doubtful gleam,
May soon extinguished be or intermitted,
With this more vivid butterfly, bright-winged,
In her triumphant and ascending course,
Presuming to compare. 'Tis rash, at least,
Audacious on our part, a foolish vaunt,
Which wisdom might reprove.

Isis.

Not what she is,
But what may be, I in the earth behold,
Her possibilities divine discern,
The bright ideal world at which she aims,
And may in her predestined course become.
Between that orb and her great prototype,
Since Mira her new era hath attained,
Deep truly would appear the gulf profound,
Almost impassable, and yet in fact,
While in essential form one they remain,

Howe'er in outward aspects various,
It may be spanned.

Hyperion.

Until that time arrives,
More manifest our wisdom will appear,
And modesty likewise, if we consent,
While still our planet's high pre-eminence,
Exists alone unhappily in hope,
Somewhat to waive the o'er-exalted claims
Put forth methinks too unadvisedly,
On her behalf.

Hesperus.

Therewith I too agree,
For like the image of a star or sun,
Reflected in a solitary pool,
Whose turbid waves but faintly reproduce
The true original ; so dim, so pale,
A faint reflection of this glorious star,
Though her ideal and fair prototype
Appears the pettier earth ; to me at least,
This plain would seem ; and what thou dost assert,
Though uttered mine own thought to justify

And startled admiration to sustain,
Has much amazed me and perplexed my mind.
For in a smaller orb, of lower rank,
I should have looked the counterpart to find,
And close companion of my native globe,
Many indeed more level with her state,
Than this sweet planet-flower, which from afar,
A copy rude and wild and tear-defaced,
She sadly imitates.   What then may be
The fundamental characters and forms
Which mark them out amid the planet realm
As thus conjoined ?

Isis.

Thine own eyes testify ;
Their light thrilled atmospheres encompassing,
In weight and density approximate ;
Their soils in kind are similar, and hence
A vegetation similar sustain,
Although more rich and varied on this globe,
More radiant far.   Nor is it otherwise
With that enormous kingdom animate,
The speechless tribes that challenge thy regard,
Whose savage and tumultuous, teeming ranks,

Though here immense the varied scale displayed
Of novel type, of shape and vivid hue,
The creatures of terrestrial origin
Greatly assimilate; while at their head,
The end and summit still of nature's toil,
Her ruling Spirit crowned with consciousness,
The happy peoples of this radiant orb,
In mind and countenance, in form and speech,
Resemble the inhabitants of earth,
Although more subtly moulded and divine,
Etherialized. The measurements of time,
Are likewise on both planets uniform,
A vital point of similarity,
But seldom found so fully emphasized,
On globes far more alike in size and rank.
For day and night, with their sweet vassal train,
The ever-glancing and delightful hours,
On either globe their rythmic changes sweet
Alike reiterate. The whirling years,
In ordered course, and the recurrent months
Their revolutions equably perform,
And so the gentle seasons alternate,
Dissolving and renewed, though here how fair
That love-linked sisterhood; the viewless God,

In his unceasing and majestic flight,
Beating on either orb with one same pulse,
From either spheral lyre eliciting,
As their resounding vibrant chords he smites,
The same response.   Their periods too remote,
Those æons dim of embryonic growth,
Of infancy and early youth unformed,
A twilight gloom of undevelopment
That endless seemed, although long since fulfilled,
Phases identical have ever marked.
One path their early peoples have pursued,
And in the steps of this transcendent race,
The nations of the earth we trust will tread.
In calmer hour serene here shalt thou come,
Hither to this irradiate realm return,
To read the storied scroll of Mira's past,
Her present with fruition crowned survey,
And muse upon thy planet's happier fate,
Beholding here, though in transfigured form,
What in a nobler future, rich in hope,
Propitious if her dawning era prove,
She may perchance become.

Hesperus.

A happy task
Which thou shalt teach me rightly to perform.
But yet sad doubts e'en now my mind assail,
For that our shadowed earth with this fair globe
Should ever vie, though in her golden prime
And high millenium bliss, ah, this to me
Impossible appears.

Isis.

Trust then our word,
Nor vex thyself with doubt and anxious thought.
So vain a dream, as to thy mind 'twould seem,
That hope is not ; nor is it well assured,
As we would wish, but dare not claim so much.
The sudden transformations that occur
In planet peoples who attain their prime,
Repeated by the race the great events
Transcendent of each soul, thou know'st not yet ;
Nor hast divined the changes marvellous
That may by evolution slow be wrought,
And gradual growth.   No race of mortal birth,
Evolved and by thy natal orb sustained,

In her existing and chaotic state,
With her most grave defects of soil and clime,
Her deserts shelterless and torrid zones,
Her frozen poles and her dead satellite,
Could e'er, 'tis true, e'en in their golden prime,
The splendid scenes displayed upon this orb
In glory reproduce.   But if mankind,
Forsaking his rude wars and futile toils,
And bending to this task imperative
The general will and the collective strength,
The shrine he dwells upon would renovate,
The blemishes of nature everywhere
Eradicate, these everywhere subdue,
And her resources and endowments rich—
Achieving on a universal scale
With efforts trained and fully organized,
What earlier centuries, inadequate,
In their imperfect fashion have begun—
Develop and enhance ; if man redeemed,
Nature, o'er which he rules, would thus redeem,
The globe entrusted him thus recreate,
The lovely earth, in her new floral bloom,
E'en this resplendent orb, e'en Mira fair,
Pursuing brightly on her humbler path

A relative perfection much the same,
Would soon approximate ; and then indeed,
The happy generation, laurel-wreathed,
Who that great victory supreme had won,
On their transfigured earth, the God thereof,
A festival like this, gorgeous, world-wide,
A planet fête of love and harmony
Might celebrate.   Or if their higher path
Of peace and wisdom they refuse to tread,
A new solution imminent may wait,
Of which thou hast not heard, the problems dark
That now perplex mankind.   For, Hesperus,
In their terrestrial shrine improvements slight,
Which scarce appreciable to thy young mind
Would seem, and yet important, fundamental,
Her soil and clime at once would modify,
Preparing thus the planet to become
The meet abode of a perfected race,
A deviation in her orbit wrought,
And trifling variation in her form,
The work of our strong arm, not of mankind,
An enterprize outreaching human strength ;
Such changes, radical although minute,
Which we have pondered on and may effect,

M

Would not improbably in one great hour,
That lovely globe completely renovate ;
Achieving for her higher destiny
And hence for her great races yet unborn,
What centuries of perilous ascent,
The slow reward of painful human toil,
Would fail at last as fully to attain ;—
Assuming now that they progressive proved,
And not the sad reverse ;—transform her quite,
Ay, send her whirling on her glowing course
A gem, a flawless pearl of orblets rare,
A rosebud in the planetary realm,
Of Mira sweet, in all her pomp and pride
The living miniature.

Hesperus.

O, glorious thought !
Conception marvellous !   But why delay ?
If from slight changes, such great good would flow,
The earth transfiguring, why hesitate
Your purpose to achieve ?   For that great cause
All enterprises less beneficent,
Less high in aim, in interest less profound,
Relinquishing ?

Aglaia.

Ah no, dream not thereof,
The fearful risk thou dost not comprehend.
For should we in our rash endeavour fail,
Our planet would be lost, wrecked fearfully,
Or might be so ; and though with triumph crowned,
The present race, their doom beyond repeal,
Would of necessity by that fell blow
Be swept away.   Therefore we hesitate,
Young Hesperus, and for that cause delay.
For in mankind great qualities exist,
Their noblest souls to daring heights ascend ;
And still we hope that those exalted minds,
The apathetic masses leavening,
Will needless render that extreme attempt ;
That they themselves, successful in their course,
With earnest effort and united toil,
Though not indeed without our powerful aid,
Will vanquish evil in that troubled world,
The sorrows that torment them now and wrongs,
High-hearted in the patient centuries,
Themselves subdue.

Hesperus.

All this to me is strange,
For as ye know, scarce from the earth returned,
Where human friends beloved my help had claimed,
On wings of flame I found myself upborne,
And swept triumphantly with viewless speed,
Of our great mission uninformed and aim,
And of the planet's course all uninformed,
Which, as 'twould seem, we came to aid and bless,
To this fair realm.   Whence wildered I appear.
More fully then these mysteries explain.
How comes it that this regal race sublime,
In glowing youth so early has attained
This high pre-eminence ? what talk is this
Of shattered globes and wrecked humanities ?
And races from that ruin new evolved ?
Of which a warning note, e'en from our throne,
Like some more dread, unlooked for thunderbolt,
That in a limpid sky reverberates,
My mind amazed ; a tempest of fierce doom,
Which, as 'twould seem, e'en now impending lowers
Terrific o'er mankind.

Hyperion.

All shalt thou learn,
Fear not, in time ; at present to thy breast
Sweet patience woo, for this of anxious thought
And disquisition sad is not the hour.
Enough that on that globe some ages since
A lower race who retrogressive proved,
Perverse, and wayward, slothful, apathetic,
Though not without high aims and aptitudes,
Much like the populations known on earth,
All too well known in fact for our content,
Unworthy found, were for their crimes destroyed ;
A hazardous and daring enterprize
On whose successful issue fortune smiled ;
For from the earlier planet, low in rank,
Imperial sprang this orb magnificent,
And from that fallen race this Phœnix bright,
Who in their rapid course and ardent youth
Most planet peoples have e'en now surpassed,
Thus early founding on their favoured globe
This kingdom fortunate, admired by all,
A Paradise reflecting heaven itself,
And yet not more divine we dare believe

Than our own planet will in time display,
When nature has attained her final form,
And man in glory has established there
Of harmony his blest estate ; the task,
Or of the present race, regenerate,
Or of the future monarch of the globe,
The nobler yet unborn Humanity
For whose high advent they and we prepare ;
Their use e'en thus fulfilled.   Let this suffice,
And feed thy fancy with these gorgeous scenes,
Enough methinks thy young mind to ensnare,
And banish thence all thought of other realms,
While here we pause.

Hesperus.

Ah, thou art right.
For here enchantment and illusion dwell.
This city fair o'er which we hovering float,
Still moving gently as the planet moves,
Enchained 'twould seem by her magnetic breath,
Her fair companions all outvying far,
How like a queen, resplendent in their midst,
Enthroned appears.   With those far-gleaming fanes,
Those towers and palaces and sculptured shrines
Enriched with ornament and strange device,

And efflorescent with ethereal bloom,
Our own celestial sphere, ay, heaven itself,
It might adorn ;—when heaven, that is, exists ;
When our bright sphere cities and towns can claim,
And shows not like the swift electric gleam
Seen on the earth on tranquil wintry nights,
And how divine !—the banner of the North,
Flung quavering o'er the zenith's broad expanse,
The lover's pledge impassioned of the pole,
Through whose auroral palpitations flash,
Like dewy eyes, love-lit, the liquid stars,
As through this roseate veil e'erwhile our heaven,
Which scarcely stains with evanescent blush,
The limpid brow of space our starry Hosts ;—
When we a heaven can boast this lovely town
A site therein distinguished might command,
How then is't named ?

Aglaia.

As should its state denote,
The planet's capital and central town,
Harmonia, the beautiful, 'tis called ;
Here stand the courts supreme whence radiate
Of wisdom pure and truth the sun-like beams,
All nations and all lands illumining,

And here the central throne, whereon sublime
Their noblest monarch reigns ; here beats at height
With full pulsation the collective pulse.
As in the bounding ocean, at high tide,
The hidden streams and currents of the deep,
The hopes and aims of this exulting hour,
From every state that flow, each zone and clime,
And from each heart on this vast globe and mind,
E'en here converge.   See how the festive streets
With grand processions and triumphal shows
Are all alive.   The happy citizens
Receive and welcome now, with open arms,
The joyous multitudes who hither flock,
The favoured guests and representatives
From other lands sent forth.

Hesperus.

Oh, wondrous scene,
What fulness unexampled of rich life,
What strength, what force, what energy divine !
Harmonia sweet, well is their city named,
For harmony and love are here enthroned,
Wisdom and peace.   The thronged and festive streets,
Show like the glowing pageant of a dream,

Intense with ecstasy at every point.
Processions grand, assembling far and near,
In splendid troops and stately cavalcades,
On prancing steeds proudly caparisoned
Careering forth ; or trampling down superb
In regiments and legions gay on foot,
In flower-strewn paths lush beds of fragrant bloom,
Or in effulgent cars in state upborne,
Most sumptuously emblazoned and adorned,
With pomp unparalleled and phantasy,
And moving rhythmical to thunder peals
Of music loud and sweet, dread harmonies
Commingling with our own celestial strains,
Storming with love and joy these heavenly spheres,
Beneath triumphal arch and glittering dome,
With floating flag and floral wreath festooned,
Incessantly—a gorgeous spectacle—
In swift succession stream.   The palaces
Wide-eyed and open-portaled with delight,
With gleaming emblems lavishly adorned,
A blaze of splendour in the morning sun,
More radiant flash soul-lit with living gems,
The brighter light divine of regal fronts
And dazzling smiles ; while in the sculptured shrines,

And temples vast with prayerful votaries thronged,
Half seen, at shadowed altars, incense-hung,
Veiled priestesses, with litany and chaunt,
Or by the sybil's holy rage inspired,
Prophetical, with strains oracular,
Their mystical solemnities and rites
Dream-like perform.   So in the city's heart,
While hill and vale and mount beyond rejoice,
Engarlanded those suburbs rich, bride-like ;
Enclustered with sweet groups of happy souls
Sheltered by tropic trees of giant growth,
Or gilded sheen of canopy and tent,
The hills on every side are garrulous ;
The plains are jubilant with ardent youth—
What grace in those young forms divine and strength !
E'en like the heroes of the early Greeks
Immortal in our Homer's living page,
Who god-like celebrate symbolic games,
And sports heroical ; and glisten starred
On every side with speeding chariots,
Self-moving that appear, electrical,
Or drawn by wondrous creatures, fabulous,
Imagined on the earth but ne'er beheld ;
White dragons, lustrous as the lightning's flash,

And clothed with thunder-bolts, so swift and dread,
And griffins, golden-scaled, and mighty winged,
Terrifical and beautiful at once,
And wingèd steeds; ambassadors who bear,
Illustrious guests and famous visitants,
Well known, from other lands. The very air,
Impalpable, with glowing life is gemmed,
Those limped fields strange vessels permeate,
As swift as dream and scintillant as flame,
Like birds immense, celestial doves or swans,
Floating serene in pure aerial streams,
In whose bedizened cars the fragrant nests
Of happy Aeronauts, bright faces smile,
There too, at dizzy heights, sweet living souls,
Who, greet, with laughter greet, their friends below,
And gems and flowers rain down as from the clouds.
The shining waters, silent, sun-becalmed,
Are souled with bird-like flocks of white-winged fleets,
Swiftly with glancing grace manœuvring,
Each ship more sumptuous than that famous barque
Where Cleopatra, goddess-like, reclined,
Not tended only by obsequious slaves,
Her vassals trained; by Venus served in state,
By Cupid dread with elemental flames,

And viewless loves.　Ah, here should Shakespeare
　　stand,
Or splendour-loving Pindar, laurel-crowned,
Or Sappho, with her pure Æolian lyre,
This vision to behold, more radiant far
Than earthly scenes on which their eyes once fed,
Though not more splendid than those poets dreamed,
And celebrate in flowing pomp of verse.

Isis.

Those lofty souls, by thy desire invoked,
Are here, doubt not, and witness this fair scene,
In their conspicuous place, 'mid these bright ranks,
Thyself in time shalt see them and demand.

Hesperus.

Each moment to my spirit brings new joy ;
An unawakened chord finds in my heart,
That lyre divine, to smite ere it be sped ;
Whose silver note to fuller utterance swells
My ceaseless hymn of gratitude and praise.

Orion.

Forget not in thy young delight, sweet youth,
　At this fair pageant and imperial show,

The higher aim these congregated spheres
That bade rejoicing to this radiant realm ;
This planet rich in bloom to vivify,
And her most noble race of lofty mould,
In their progressive, beatific path,
Ascending still, to bless and consecrate ;
With wisdom from on high illuming
Each soul, amid the happy multitudes,
On whom we gaze.   To this task bend thy mind,
For thou dost share with these assembled Hosts
In whose commingled Consciousness and Will,
The Will of the Eterne expression finds,
Their grace celestial and beatitude ;
The youngest born in heaven, our life is thine,
By one great purpose animated all,
Nor from the duties of thy new estate,
Responsibilities sublime and claims,
Canst thou escape.

Hesperus.

Since o'er this globe we float,
Such benediction and celestial grace,
As from this feeble breast can emanate,

Upon this race by me has been breathed forth
With ceaseless flow.

Aglaia.

We see it, gentle youth,
Yet for thy counsel, fair Orion, thanks.
A timely warning and suggestion wise
That all should heed ; for now the sacred hour
Which will from these united Hosts exact,
Absorbed therewith our whole collective strength,
A special effluence of balm-breathing love,
And stimulating thought, draws swiftly near.
The planet's potentates, e'en while we speak,
Hither by their momentous mission drawn,
Prepare to meet.   From fair Harmonia's courts,
The long processions in unending files,
With banners gay and symbols rich unfurled,
With volleying thunders of artillery,
The blast and blare of loud-voiced instruments,
And hymnings sweet of votive choristers,
Innumerous as sunset pageantries,
In splendid state proceed.   The joyous youth,
Assembled on the plains forget their sports,
And range themselves in well-appointed ranks,

Or haste a place conspicuous to assume ;
The hills and mounts send down swift streams of souls,
And grow attentive in the clustered groups
Still lingering on those heights.   A sudden shock,
A thrill of inexpressible delight,
Each soul in that vast multitude has stirred,
Like that which glows and tingles in each nerve,
When some great joy the beating of the heart
Accelerates.   To one point all converge,
To that great centre flow in ordered ranks,
Or bend thereon a rapt, attentive gaze,
The sacred shrine, the temple beautiful,
In which e'en now the planet's ruling minds
Assembling congregate.

Hesperus.

A marvel new,
That miracle of art now first I note,
Which viewed the soul of the whole scene appears.
With one vast gem, a fount of azure light,
Sky-like endomed ; with floating draperies hung,
A moving veil of soft ethereal shapes,
Like clouds or mists that of the setting sun,
Wind-wafted to the west have deeply quaffed,

A heaven beneath the limpid vault on high,
By rows of light-emitting shafts upheld,
Pillars majestical, its sole support,
Each, each, a lustrous and translucent stone,
Some precious gem, opals and emeralds,
Huge amethysts and rubies, diamonds, pearls,
Brightening the day with their contrasted flames,
How fair it stands on yon selected plain,
The broad expanse of consecrated ground,
Whereon appears, sequestered and apart,
No lesser fane or meaner habitation,
For that transcendent monument reserved;
That shrine of shrines.　At stated intervals,
By lofty trees, cloud-visited engirt,
Than palm-trees tall far more majestical,
Like watchful sentinels at a king's gate,
Not meant the guarded treasure to conceal,
But by their presence indicate its worth,
Lo, how it blazes, meteor-like, and flames,
Most flawless fair in perfect symmetry,
And wonderful in wealth of ornament;
Like some far-visioned temple of the sun,
Or living planet fount, original,
Of holy light.　Thereon all eyes are fixed,

And open as the day, all unenclosed,
With gleaming vistas marvellous and aisles
With all their treasures rich and rare displayed,
In calm security and confidence,
As bountiful as such a fane should stand,
Free to the zephyrs mild that visit it,
And gaze of the enraptured multitudes,
That ravished contemplation it invites ;
Magnificent.   The temple of a world,
The sanctuary blest of all the lands,
Selected by the peoples, far and wide,
To hearken in its first impassioned flight
A happy generation's hymn of praise,
The aspirations and collective prayers,
The new-winged hopes and infinite desires,
Heaven-soaring of a race.   Lo, swiftly now,
Assembling the appointed potentates,
'Tis filled with haughty waves of splendid life,
As by a rising flood impetuous
E'en to its full capacity o'erflown ;
The silence hushed and solemn solitude,
That reigned e'erwhile within those precincts vast,
Dispelled by that insurging swelling tide,
Vanish and disappear, like fleeing Night,

When quaffs the golden Dawn with sudden smile
Her chalice of obscurity, star-wreathed ;
As darkness flees from day's inflowing beams.
The Congress meets, those high Ambassadors,
Grand Embassies and regal Convocations,
Their places and appointed seats assume
And glittering thrones. Conspicuous in their midst,
In yon most gracious form, majestical,
Erect upon the Temple's central throne,
The gem-encrusted heart of that vast gem,
We see no doubt the monarch of the realm,
And in the radiant vision by his side,
That soft resplendence feminine—ah, both,
In loveliness how peerless, grace and charm,
How wise and mild those light enhaloed brows,
Its fair and happy queen.

Procyon.

'Tis as thou sayst,
And more those names of sovereign state imply,
Than thou, so newly from the earth upborne,
Perchance mayst deem. In yon immortal twain,
Not only king and queen dost thou behold,
But therewithal the mind most luminous,

The spirit most sublime, most pure and true,
Amid the children multitudinous
Of this great globe ; prophet and king at once,
Poet and seer, with wisdom crowned serene,
Genius and grace.   For in a world so blest,
'Mid peoples thus exalted, cultured, wise,
The nature of each being is revealed,
And each assuming his appropriate place,
His true vocation found, his pathway known,
His god-appointed destiny fulfils.
Apollo's lyre the lyric poet grasps,
The peaceful herdsman guards his tranquil flocks,
The soldier meets the brunt of fearful war,
Waged to preserve the race and not destroy,
With nature waged, with death and pestilence,
With fate, corrupting crime, with haggard want
And misery ; in this sense soldiers all,
Whate'er their special calling and pursuit,
Since all alike stand pledged, in time of need,
The public weal to guard, a sacred trust,
Which at the sacrifice of life itself,
Each soul in such a cause heroical,
All would fulfil ;—the scholar seeks his books,
And pleasures sparkling draught the sybarite ;

And he upon whose sacred head is placed
A nation's highest gift, the mystic crown,
The golden symbol of authority,
By right divine of his own virtue rules,
His noble nature's bright supremacy,
This, this alone the signet from on high,
Impressed on regal and anointed brows;
The consecrating oil vouchsafed to kings
By heaven ordained.　In yon resplendent shrine,
Assembled thus in fellowship and love
Their destined task momentous to achieve,
Before thee stands a congregation blest,
The flower of virtue and of intellect,
Summoned from all the states and happy lands,
The noblest souls upon the planet known;
Monarchs and lovely queens, and Emperors,
Philosophers and poets, statesmen, seers,
The student pale for learning deep renowned,
The sage revered, with wisdom crowned and age,
And by his side, with lightning glance of youth,
And daring brow, the favourite of the Muse,
By sacred gifts oracular inspired,
The mind, the soul, the spirit of the race,
A Convocation most magnificent.

Hesperus

Upon the earth it would not be believed.
For there, the most progressive minds and free,
With monarchs are at war, rank would o'erthrow,
And in its place equality enforce,
Deeming that freedom can be found alone
In plain, republican simplicity,
There virtue only found and true content.
And this mine own ideal was I own,
Which here most strangely falsified I find.
For 'mid these peoples virtuous and wise,
Immense variety of rank exists,
Imposing state, proud splendour, pomp, display ;
Our human seers, our statesmen, writers, chiefs,
The best and wisest on that planet known,
Such wealth, such happiness, prosperity,
For their more abject race would fear to claim,
And from such splendour shrink.

Hyperion.

Too sluggish flows
In their dull veins the glowing vital stream,
For pomp and wealth, for luxury and state,

To noble spirits these are benefits,
The wings of light outspread on which they soar,
The measure of their duties and their claims,
Responsibilities and privilege ;
The weaker nature only they degrade,
Languid, inert, and to corruption prone,
The sensual soul.   Nor is equality,
Truly interpreted, to rank opposed,
To station and to wealth inimical,
But rests thereon as on a pedestal,
Without whose firm support shattered 'twould fall,
A wrecked ideal.   Variety of rank,
In all her realms and kingdoms infinite,
Nature herself has everywhere ordained,
Nor could in any world, the simplest soul,
Most humble in vocation and pursuit,
Most limited in intellect and scope,
His petty meed of culture due obtain,
Or happiness enjoy, save in and through
The higher lives of beings more sublime,
That o'er his own existence towering rise,
Fulfilled in their perfection his desire,
In their achievement merged his aspiration,
As in his service are their needs fulfilled,

No vicious circle this, sophistical,
But that of life.   Of every planet orb,
The children multitudinous are one,
In aim and destiny allied they stand,
As of a forest the majestic growths,
Or in a system, intricate and vast,
The whirling orbs.   The rulers of the lands,
On this transcendent globe, the high in rank,
From their devoted subjects, fortunate,
Tribute well worthy of the name receive ;
Love, admiration, reverence and faith,
The grateful incense wafted to their thrones
From every heart and homestead in the states
O'er which they mildly rule ; while they in turn
Upon their subjects sacred gifts confer,
Welfare assured, prosperity and peace,
Content in all their ranks and happiness,
Ay, and a higher boon ; with lofty aims
With pure desires and aspirations pure,
They rouse and animate their ardent minds,
An effluence of energy divine
Transmitting from their central seat of power,
That permeates with vivifying force,
Each creature dwelling in their broad domains ;

This interchange of life perpetual,
Repeating in the social commonwealth,
The ebb and flow of prayer and benefaction,
Of love in yearning known and in fruition,
The creature and creator that unite,
As in the Heavenly Hosts.   Deem not o'er all,
Upon this favoured planet unenjoyed
The tranquil pleasures and serene delights
Which thou and justly so dost venerate,
The sole true basis of the common weal,
In every sphere alike immutable ;
From whose exhaustless depth, their living source—
As from the ocean's fathomless profound,
The passing pageantry of mist and cloud—
Such scenes as this of beautiful display,
Demanded by the festive hour arise ;
Evoked and consecrated when evoked,
By general joys and universal aims,
The full accords of perfect harmony,
Unknown upon the earth and unconceived,
But which henceforward on this radiant orb,
Not quenching lower joys, fulfilling them,
Will constantly prevail.   In this high hour,
Fair Mira in her festive garb thou seest,
Arrayed e'en like a queen to celebrate,

Forget it not, the dawn of her new day,
Her brighter golden age.

Aglaia.

Peace now, I pray.

For all things mark in expectation stand.
The countless troops of beaming seraphim,
Who sped erewhile that glowing orb to bless,
Lovely, to their celestial spheres return ;
How sweet, ah me, how sweet the mystic songs,
Re-echoed to and fro from heaven to heaven,
Which fill and overflow with harmony
These gleaming plains.   They heed us not below,
Know not how much their higher life depends
Upon the viewless and electric streams
That from these radiant spheres impalpable
Upon their globe are shed.   It matters not,
More dear they seem in their young innocence,
May every living soul whom we behold,
Be thrilled and quickened with celestial grace.
Ah, happy hour.

*The Angelic Groups in all the heavens grow silent and
attentive, observing what occurs in the planet beneath.
The Seraphim who have been hovering over the globe
return to their respective spheres.*

Hymn of Seraphim.

How fair !   O, fairer than a full-blown flower
          It blooms,
Gemmed with the dews of love, and rich with dower
          Of sweet perfumes.
          How balmy is the air !
An incense of high hope in this great hour
          Breathes everywhere.

How sweet !   O, sweetest joy that angels know,
          When thus
The hearts and minds of men responsive glow
          Inspired by us :
          What rich reward and rare,
To see the seed we tend and water grow,
          And blossom fair.

Behold them now this great and glorious race !
          Since first
Their sires bade war to holy peace give place,
          What flowers have burst
          Upon this garden scene ;
Wild weeds and barren wastes no more we trace
          But all is green.

See what a silver kiss the sun hath set
        In love
On yon fair Temple's dome, where now are met
        New plans to move,
      Their sages of renown ;
Which shall to all a brighter era yet
        Of peace hand down.

The city beautiful of hill and vale
        Below,
In grace and in the grandeur of its scale
        Hath more to show
      Than outward forms of art,
Though bright as visions which in fairy tale
        To life upstart.

Those stately palaces, those temples chaste,
        Those domes,
Which rise magnifical and amply spaced ;
        Those shapely homes
      Whence labour's humble train
Come forth, declare ease, comfort, wealth, and taste
        A common gain.

But more, this wealth of grandeur doth present
　　　　A type
And reflex of the mind's development,
　　　　Whose instincts ripe
　　　　With love of beauty thrill,
Divine, by self-indulgence only bent
　　　　Aside to ill.

But now how fair a field do we behold
　　　　And clear ;
No rocks or thorns, which late the soil did hold,
　　　　Now interfere
　　　　To kill free labour's seed ;
But where they sow one level plain of gold
　　　　Shall soon succeed.

Una.

Let silence reign in heaven's eternal courts,
The planet's potentates, rulers and seers,
In solemn conclave now assembled meet,
New laws and customs new to ratify,
And 'mid rejoicing pæans, far and wide,
Their golden age of harmony and love
Inaugurate. Lo, hearken their discourse,
While breathing on the convocation vast

Assembled in yon temple beautiful,
The effluent fulness of the life divine.

Silence in all the Hosts, the Angels bestowing their attention upon the Miranite Congress assembled in the Temples below. The Choruses are intermitted. The Monarch of Harmonia, the principal city of the globe, addresses the Convocation.

Monarch of Harmonia.

Monarchs of our great dominion, here assembled in
    your pride,
Rulers of the happy nations, leaders of the lands allied,
First and foremost, ye, the aged, seers and prophets,
    wise, sublime,
And scarce less for wisdom noted, in maturity's full
    prime,
Ye the bulwark of your kingdoms, suns of righteous-
    ness and truth,
And ye too in starry splendour, glowing ranks of
    ardent youth,
One and all, whate'er your nation, station and vocation,
    power,
Greetings from our Throne receive;—welcome all in
    this great hour.

Where triumphant we assemble, favoured, fortunate, caressed,

Scarce a cycle since our fathers met with heavy hearts opprest,

Met in doubt and fear to grapple with the woes that racked the world,

Met to quell them, to subdue them ; here the flag of peace unfurled.

Wrongs unnumbered, teeming, thronging, vanished at their high decree,

As the mists of night from morning they beheld them fade and flee,

Superstition, false ambition, ignorance, and hate and fear,

These they slew, with aim united, armed and fearful with truth's spear,

And therewith fierce war abolished, root of crime in every land,

Root of discord, of perdition, foremost of the demon band,

From whose grave, unwept, unhallowed, lovely sprang the tree of peace,

Neath whose shadow harvests blooming through the endless years increase,

Harvests which 'tis ours to garner in our ripe and happy
    day,
Fruitful fields of law and order, rich as meadows sweet
    of May.
Glory to those noble heroes, peace and honour to each
    name,
For each brow a wreath immortal, worthy each of
    deathless fame,
Whose great faith that deed accomplished, by whose
    toil those fields were sown,
In the hope with full fruition their posterity to
    crown,
To transmit to their descendants, seeking in each age
    new life,
The alliance of the nations, freed for evermore from
    strife.
This the heritage they conquered, this the glory of
    the morn,
Whose effulgent noon unclouded, we transmit to those
    unborn,
To our children, our descendants handing down,
    for ever blest,
The great gift of love and freedom, of this age the
    high behest.

Lo, stand forth ye calm-browed sages, speak sweet
  poets debonnaire,
Speak, the welfare of the peoples in your place and
  rank declare ;
This avouch, and more exalted, with glad prophecy
  reveal,
Of the future the new promise, the new hope this
  hour shall seal ;
Speak, declare, uplift your voices, let your happy
  strains resound,
And forget not in your anthems—sacred still those
  names renowned—
O, forget not to our fathers to award our grateful
  praise,
And pure worship reverential to the Author of our
  days.

Herald.

Statesmen, potentates and seers,
Princely all 'mid princely peers,
Hearkening to your monarch's voice,
Bid our splendid groups rejoice,
Hearkening to the uttered word
Of your king, your chief and lord,

On whose brow heaven's lightnings gleam,
Crowned with wisdom, loved, supreme ;
Spokesmen of the nations rise,
Let us hear 'neath watchful skies
Tidings of each happy land.
Speak ; obey the great command.

*A representative Statesman, Ambassador of the various
kingdoms of the planet, is first to respond to the
greeting of the King of Harmonia.*

The Nations.

When the nations, a cycle ago, sought the kingdom
of virtue and grace,
When they stood heart to heart unafraid, hand in
hand, when they met face to face,
Like goddesses fair, light-crowned, or the Muses with
resonant lyres,
Gentle peace sought the altars of war and quenched
with her weeping their fires,
And the fiend fled afar with his train, wild lusts
and unbridled desires.

Then the reign of violence ceased, and the peoples
discordant drew breath,

o

Clear daylight not yet had they found, but a pause
   and a respite from death,
And they trembled as though in a dream, fear-stricken,
   and fevered with care,
In each breast the gnawings of hunger, the rendings of
   want and despair,
For poverty still in each nation and sin like wild beasts
   made their lair.

But now freed from warfare external, the statesmen
   and spirits of light,
Arose, to contend with those demons, unshackled,
   in terrible might,
And they quelled them with ease in each land, and
   banished in terror afar;
Wild-eyed, in haggard confusion, they fled in the
   wake of fierce war,
And smiled o'er the purified peoples the dawn with
   her tremulous star.

Now pæans arose of thanksgiving, rejoicings, and
   anthems of praise,
The temples of law and of order and peace were
   upreared in those days,

The ravaging armies of old disappeared with war-
    fare and crime,
But legions and troops of redemption went forth upon
    missions sublime,
Of the peoples collective the will to fulfil in the
    fulness of time.

In the service of art and religion and science went
    forth in their pride
Industrial armies undaunted, sent out by the nations
    allied,
And marvels ere long they effected, achievements
    unparalleled wrought,
New kingdoms and statutes established, with chaos
    unterrified fought,
And e'en from the ends of creation rich trophies of
    victory brought.

The deserts they dauntless invaded and vanquished the
    stifling simoon,
Arid wastes were replaced by rich gardens rewarding
    their labour full soon.
In the boreal seas they adventured and conquered the
    kingdoms of ice,

Their weapons were patience and faith, perseverance
and zeal, sacrifice,
And wherever they trod their presence created a fair
Paradise.

Thus was nature redeemed and adorned, thus embel-
lished our beautiful globe,
With bloom and fertility garnished, with verdure thus
clad as a robe,
Of disease no longer was seen the pallid and suffering
face,
But death like an angel enfolded the old in a tranquil
embrace,
And lovelier far grew the peoples, transformed and
transfigured the race.

The cities, once haunts of perdition, where poverty,
ignorance, shame,
With luxury walked in alliance, unhallowed their
union and fame,
Released from those deep-rooted evils, corruptions and
follies avowed,
In splendour conspicuous blazed like the sun bursting
forth from a cloud,

Of all ranks and classes and orders the virtue and
honour allowed.

Fair centres of knowledge and wisdom, illustrious,
wealthy, renowned,
They dazzled all eyes with their beauty, with temples
and palaces crowned,
And sorrow and want in their precincts and crime
henceforth were unknown ;
No dungeon ill-omened or fortress the sunshine obscured with their frown,
No culprit was found in those cities, no statute or
law was o'erthrown.

In each populous kingdom and state, in clusters and
groups without end,
O'er the length and the breadth of the globe those
visions of glory extend,
Proportioned in numbers and size, and linked by a
common command,
Control in the cities, dominion, and peace in the
fair village band,
And the streams and currents of life in their veins flow
on through each land,

In union regenerate thus, like palm trees the nations
    now stood,

A grove of majestical palms, a sacred and fair sisterhood.

And as lowly bushes and blooms at the foot of tall
    trees make their bed,

The peoples more feeble and small by the strong were
    nourished and fed,

O'er their weakness dependent in love a roof of pro-
    tection outspread.

Thus, thus have they sped in the past, since that high
    immemorial hour,

'Till sublime in the present they stand fulfilled in
    virtue and power,

As stars from a mountain beheld the nations illustrious
    shine,

Each land is a temple of peace and each kingdom of
    wisdom a shrine ;

While the peoples expectant in glory await the Era
    divine.

Herald.

Clothed with honour, virtue, power,
Magnates of this radiant hour,

Priests of Freedom, Truth, and Love,
The great Trinity above,
Obedient to your monarch's will
Your sacred mission now fulfil.
Spokesmen in your glory rise,
Let us hear 'neath bending skies,
Fostered by the general heart,
Tidings blest of Faith and Art,
And the latest verity
Of science and philosophy,
Tell us of the growth of mind,
Free, progressive, unconfined,
Tell us what our noble race,
Sanctified by love and grace,
In the happy past has won,
What remains to do, undone ;—
Swell aloud our name and fame,
Each his oracle proclaim.

*The second call of the Herald is responded to by
a Seer and Ambassador representing the various
Sciences, after whom speak in succession the representatives of Philosophy, of Literature and Art, and of
Religion.*

Science.

The vanquished sphinx her secrets doth reveal,
   Her mysteries obediently disclose,
From science naught presuming to conceal,
    In action or repose.

Persistently and long with searching glance,
   We peer beneath her many folded veil,
And feed unwearied on her countenance,
    With our own ardour pale.

We walk though planet bound with god-like tread,
   The elements and tempests know our face,
Amid the stars is reared our awful head,
    And lost in viewless space.

Those moving orbs we analyze and weigh,
   Where'er their winged splendours throb and blaze,
We marshal them in their divine array,
    In many a lambent maze.

The races who inhabit them likewise,
   To science in their varied lives are known,

Their customs and their laws we scrutinize,
  Great knowledge is our crown.

And with some beings of transcendent mould,
  The last achievement of progressive time,
Communion with responsive joy we hold,
  And intercourse sublime.

O'erbridged and mastered by the toil of years
  The gulf that yawned between us though immense
We greet athwart the voids our planet peers
  With ecstasy intense.

Though baffled long we seemed, that path of light
  We patiently have reared, our crowning deed,
Of all our labours in a past so bright,
  This, this the glorious meed.

Such proud achievements science can proclaim,
  Such triumphs and such victories narrate,
Beloved and feared she stands, a dreaded name,
  Supreme o'er time and fate.

And yet the conquests of enduring thought,
  O'er nature our supernal victories,

With rich results to all and blessings fraught,
  Our ripe discoveries.

Are but the first step in a grand ascent,
  Whose sunny heights unscaled transfigured beam,
The bow of promise there for ever bent
  With storm-subduing gleam.

Still on the ladder's lower rounds we stand,
  And see before us in a day of light,
The stations leading in our promised land,
  On through the infinite.

*The Seer of Science, having been warmly applauded
and congratulated retires, and is followed by the
Spokesman of the Students and Philosophers.*

Philosophy.

Philosophy flies through the pure upper skies to the
  mansions serene of bliss,
Where lovelily bright dwell the spirits of Light in the
  cloudless realms of day,
There freed from suspense, with joy intense, she receives of wisdom the kiss,

Ethereal balm and heavenly calm inbreathing our
   doubts to allay.

The treasures untold which science so bold ingathers
   from nature and fate,
Her tribute most sweet, are laid at her feet by subjects
   with loyal appeal,
Those glittering troops, those systems and groups her
   glance doth coordinate,
All knowledges vast of the present and past she sanc-
   tions and seals with her seal.

In her paths serene we garner and glean the fruits
   delicious of mind,
In that world intense, freed from passion and sense,
   from tempests external and flaws,
Sweet fruits and flowers as speed the soft hours we
   gather and garner and bind,
And patiently solve and subtly evolve enigmas and
   dogmas and laws.

In the earlier years when sorrows and fears oppressed
   and bewildered our race,
As oil on the wave when wild tempests rave fell softly
   the light of her smile,

She walked through the strife of that younger life, a
    spirit of patience and grace,
Chaunting low the strains that in heavenly plains
    have power the soul to beguile.

But in the new age that soon shall assuage the wrongs
    in the sad past bewailed,
Her countenance pale whence falleth the veil sun-like,
    in resplendence doth blaze ;
Enthroned and in state she goes forward elate new
    kingdoms to seize unassailed,
And to every heart rich gifts doth impart, a queen in
    these golden days.

*The Ambassador of the Philosophers having in his turn
    received the congratulations of the Assembly, is followed
    by the Representative of the Arts and of Literature.*

Art.

We all are brother sons of Art,
All Priests of Beauty we ;
    One is the worship of our heart,
Although its forms be free :
    We walk the world with eyes divine,
We see with more than common sight,

Strange music thrills our senses fine ;
We scent a fragrance fairy-light ;
    And then, inspired by angel's touch,
We give our visions to the day,
    In tints of gold, or sculpture bold,
Or music of immortal lay.

    But little heed had Beauty's face
Amid the cannon's roar ;
    It ill beseemed the limbs of grace
To paint in crimson gore ;
    Long centuries of war and need
Had all but hushed the poet's lyre ;
    The fruits of peace were gone to feed
Th' insatiate maw of sword and fire :
    And men of stern religious mood
Broke Beauty's image in her fane ;
    They could not bear a sight so fair
In such a world of woe and pain.

    But since the dove-borne olive bough
Declared war's ebbing flood,
    With steadier hand and calmer brow
Our rites have been pursued.

Rich Plenty rising from the waste
Hath showered her gifts on Beauty's shrine,
　　And Leisure lent a light to Taste,
And peasants bowed to Art divine.
　　By Learning and Religion nursed,
Henceforth unto the end of Time
　　Fair Art shall grow, and all shall know
That love of beauty is sublime.

The Ambassador of Art is likewise warmly congratu-
lated, and yields his place to the Seer of Truth and
Religion.

Religion.

As one who rapt with loving eye and tender,
　　Waiting a figure dearer than the rest,
Sees, and pursues it through a maze of splendour,
　　Secretly watching o'er it, unconfessed ;

With such an eye and heart of such devotion
　　Followed we Truth, undazzled by the throng,
Watching her sober mien and gentle motion,
　　Ready to rescue her from slight or wrong :

Tempted in vain by gaudier attractions,
  Courted unmoved by beauty and by wit;
Fancy's wild flights and science cold abstractions,
  Failing alike her modest grace to hit.

Oft was she lost, yet never once forsaken,
  Forms in half-lights her semblance would assume,
These would we follow for a while mistaken,
  Like phantom lights misleading in the gloom.

Meekly of yore she moved and little heeded,
  Mostly with doubt regarded or disdain;
While all the worth and purity they needed
  With simple grace she offered to the vain.

But in calm hours by charm of gentle merit
  Soon she prevailed to banish each conceit;
Science and Art soon panted to inherit
  Draughts of her spirit, sitting at her feet.

As in a hive whene'er the Queen Bee chances
  To make a progress through her busy race,
They drop their tasks and front as she advances,
  Greeting her presence with a loyal face.

Even such homage unto Truth they render
   Owning her royalty of nature's right ;
Painters and poets to her service tender
   All the rare gifts of colour and delight.

Nature and Art are sisters now and science
   Walks with Religion twin-like hand in hand ;
Purified faiths are joined in sweet alliance ;
   Progress and peace go smiling up the land.

Herald.

Happy in your lowly state,
Sheltered from the storms of fate,
Fulfilling in a tranquil round,
Humble duties, gladly bound,
Simple lowly, virtuous wise,
By the universal ties
Which all natures know and feel,
Source to all of woe and weal ;
Spokesmen of the peoples rise,
Let us hear 'neath watchful skies
Tidings of the joy and strife,
Tidings of the tranquil life,

Of the many ;—rich in grace ;
Happy children of our race,
The contented, busy legions,
Gathered from all lands and regions ;
Who with ceaseless toil sustain
Of sweet peace the fruitful reign ;
On the people's truth and health,
Reared and based our commonwealth,
This alone in every nation,
This of freedom the foundation.

The call of the Herald is responded to by the Ambas-
sador of the Agriculturalists, representing the Masses
of the Peoples.

Agriculture.

Prolific smiles beneath our happy toil
   Our planet fair—a mother's generous breast,
We sow with varied seed her fruitful soil,
   Thence draw our sustenance, there find our rest.

The gentle seasons pass and reappear,
   With soft entwining arms like sisters sweet,
They lead us onward through each happy year,
   With changeful smile and deftly glancing feet.

P

When Spring comes laughing forth and with gay flowers
　　The carpet trims that blooms beneath her tread,
We crown with labour the productive hours,
　　And from each bounding breast all care seems fled.

In Summer's splendid bloom and fragrant prime,
　　When like a queen she sits, a full-blown rose,
With wanton wreaths we deck the brow of time,
　　And oft in wood and woodland seek repose.

Then like a god comes Autumn calm and strong,
　　Vine-wreathed, and laden with his bursting sheaves,
When our ripe fields we reap with harvest song,
　　And each glad homestead priceless wealth receives,

But in the pause that follows, calm, sedate,
　　When droop at Winter's breath the flowrets fair,
Reposing like our fields we watch and wait,
　　And for the New Year's effort new prepare.

The rich and great, our rulers whom we love,
　　Delighted mark our fields and fertile lands ;
The kingdom they command, where'er they rove,
　　In full perfection 'neath their gaze expands.

In nature's bloom and beauty they rejoice,
　But see her not nor worship with our eyes ;
For in the wind we hear a mother's voice,
　A mother's roof behold in bending skies.

The beauty of the planet is our pride,
　Our strength our toil has made her thus divine,
Our arms have thus adorned her like a bride,
　And for her rulers decked their radiant shrine,

Nor would we with great kings our place exchange,
　Nor change with theirs our lives of calm content,
Our freedom o'er the hills and vales to range,
　Our happy toil, our rest, our ravishment.

Yet we too love of truth the countenance,
　And while swift speeding time doth onward flow,
In our own path would ceaselessly advance,
　In wisdom climb, in grace and virtue grow.

From this firm basis, well assured and calm,
　We wait the revelations yet to be,
New freedom to be won, and heavenly balm,
　The fuller strains divine of harmony.

Herald.

Everywhere is joy and love,
Hovering spirits o'er us move,
Every heart with rapture thrilled,
All things now in peace fulfilled,
Only we await, intense,
In a pause of hushed suspense,
Only we await the voice—
Seraphs at that strain rejoice—
Throned beneath the Temple's sheen,
Of our lady and our queen,
Fair Harmonia's hope and pride,
Sovereign of the lands allied.

Queen of Harmonia.

Welcome to our guests exalted, who the higher
truth embrace,
Unto all our salutation, from our throne, love, peace,
and grace ;
In this Temple bright assembled, regal, in majestic
state,
Laws harmonic to establish, new decrees to promul-
gate,

Who expectant stand before me, prince and poet, sage
    and seer,
Ardent in this day of glory—lo! transfigured ye ap-
    pear,
Whose effulgent star is rising clear and cloudless in
    the East,
Lovely queens and splendid monarchs, welcome to our
    city's feast.
Sweet, how sweet the hymns exulting that have
    charmed the listening air,
Oracles of every altar tidings jubilant declare,
Firmly based on law and order every government is
    blest,
Every land, secure and peaceful, tastes the sabbath of
    her rest,
Healed long since the harsh dissensions of an age of
    woe and strife,
Pressing onward, on and upward, seeking still new
    truth, new life,
Banded in a firm alliance, in the fulness ripe of
    time,
They await the revelation of a cycle more sublime.
Science of sustained endeavour and achievement tells
    the tale,

And philosophy, truth's priestess, from her brow uplifts
the veil,

Art has filled the world with beauty, visions of the pure
ideal,

In their loveliness eternal, in their truth and grandeur
real,

These indeed most truly real, since they vanquish death
and time,

In a world of change and shadow telling of a change-
less clime,

Sculpture in pure form embodies, marble pure, immortal dreams,

Painting writes his gorgeous legends with the sun's
prismatic beams,

Architecture tells the secret, breathes the shapely
mystery,

Crystalized in dome and nave, of monumental
symmetry ;

With sweet tones ecstatic music shrines more vast and
temples rears,

Tones of passion, deep emotion, interblended joys and
fears,

The expressionless expressing, rapture, anguish, keen
delight,

Sense and nature both transcending, yearnings of the
    infinite ;
While of that rapt Muse, the sister, poetry, with
    frenzy fired,
In the sacred garb of language, with her lyre of speech
    inspired,
Even thus of God and nature the deep secrets doth
    declare,
And the innermost unuttered in her rhythmic word lay
    bare,
Clouded else the inward vision faith, religion doth un-
    seal,
And the Infinite, Eternal, to the finite mind re-
    veal,
To the loving finite creature shows the fount, the
    source of Love,
Providential shows the Spirit, patient as the brooding
    dove.
Once these systems in dark ages their own aims and
    names belied,
False in teaching, vain and futile, harsh, dissentient,
    disallied.
Science fettered, downward gazing, with her own vast
    treasures clogged,

Pale philosophy bewildered in fantastic mists befogged,
Art devoid of aspiration, frivolous, a soulless form,
Faith by dogmas vain deluded, vexed with theologic
    storm,
Or by superstition lighted, burning with a bitter flame,
With a heart of persecution, sweet religion but in
    name ;
Thus discordant, warring, hostile, in a weary, wasteful
    round,
Aimlessly they whirled and barren in a vicious circle
    bound.
Now sustaining each the other in sweet union beatific,
In their varied realms progressive, rich and fruitful,
    free, prolific,
One in aim and faith and purpose, wreathed with
    laurel, wreathed with bay,
Passing through triumphal arches, they attain our
    brighter day :—
Happy too in every nation are proclaimed the
    multitudes,
O'er their busy ranks and orders dove-eyed peace
    serenely broods,
Voices sweet of humble labour echoing on from hill
    and vale,

Of content and satisfaction tell in every land the tale,

All is well, ye happy peoples, lo! repeat the glad
    refrain,

Tell it to the hills and mountains, swell O swell the
    blissful strain,

While your leaders in this Temple in this consecrated
    shrine,

Labour now in full communion to ordain the life
    divine,

While we now in full communion, sanctified by
    heavenly grace,

Ratify our holy Era for the Universal race,

Hence rejoice and in your pleasures O forget not to
    give praise

To our noble predecessors and the Author of our
    Days.

*As the Queen of Harmonia concludes her speech the
draperies that have been floating over the roof of the
Temple Beautiful descend, enclosing it like a solid
wall of opal. The Congress is hidden from view, the
peoples resume their interrupted sports and converse, and the choruses reawaken in the Heavenly
spheres.*

Chorus in Heaven.

Shed down, celestial Legions, on this regenerate
    race,
Assembled in their glory, the balm of heavenly
    grace.
And may their prayer aspiring to that pure source
    ascend,
On wing of praise upwafted that o'er us all doth bend,
Attaining thus impassioned the dread Eternal Throne,
And may the God Eternal their hopes and yearnings
    crown.

Hesperus.

With what deep sympathy,
What admiration, wonder and delight,
My heart is stirred.   Would that upon the earth
Some poet might arise able to pierce
With daring vision that dull atmosphere,
And view in dream prophetical this scene !
Whose cheering voice and thunder-peal of song
Those sorrow laden souls oppressed and sad,
Might to new life awake !—reveal to them—
To their great destiny so derelict,

Who so dishonour in their shameful course,
The great Creator and the Cosmic Whole—
The splendours of the living Universe,
In which with all their faults a part divine
They might perform !—why do they linger thus ?
Why thus delay their upward path to tread ?
Athwart the gulf profound that severs us,
Would that my voice might reach them and arouse !
Reach to the soul and spirit of mankind,
Persuading them the reign of holy peace,
Like this blest people to inaugurate,
Preparing for the fuller harmony
Which on that basis, that foundation sure,
A later age might rear !   O, would that it might be !
Or through some soul still living could I speak,
A human instrument still living find,
Through whom these mysteries I might declare,
And all inspire !

Hyperion.

Peace, child importunate !
Thus still to thine own loss preoccupied
And petulant with thy poor planet's fate,
Silence I say ; for now a fuller tide

Of life and glory than thy new-born soul,
Unfledged and raw, has dreamed of or conceived,
Will shake thee from thy clinging memories,
The sensual mists scatter for evermore
Which darken and perplex the feeble mind
That of existence in its endless forms,
But one poor phase has known ;—these dissipate,
And open in its fulness on thy soul,
In all its grandeur dread, Eternity,
The Absolute, the Infinite, Supreme ;—
Lo, silence then, and with suspended breath
The revelation most appalling wait,
And most sublime, which e'en in heaven itself,
Thou shalt behold, for that with trembling heart,
In fear prepare.

Isis.

Ay, Hesperus prepare.
For hither now, life's pure effulgence streams,
Down-pressing on our souls.   The living God,
Eternal, infinite, in pomp appears,
In his essential glory manifest,
Whose presence thy weak frame will scarce endure ;
Collect thyself ; prepare.

Aglaia.

Ah, God, 'tis true.

This breathless silence, inexpressible,
Which suddenly the atmosphere pervades,
This hushed suspense, this pause ineffable,
Can from one cause alone, but one proceed.
A palpitating radiance filleth space,
A glory of essential light and flame,
Which from all sides inflowing, swift and clear,
The light o'erpowers of these effulgent spheres,
As we outlustre with our potent gleam
Great Nature's lamps, the ever-whirling suns,
Whose splendours in our brighter presence pale :
The Love Eterne, the central Source of Life,
The Uncreated on his awful throne,
O'er these responsive Hosts immediate broods,
Upon each soul his effluent life is shed,
Ah God, ah God, I faint with ecstasy.

Chorus.

What glories insupportable, what ecstasies supreme,
What splendours inconceivable now from the God-head
　　stream—

Enduring scarce our bliss, O God, we tremble 'neath
  thy gaze,
We veil our blanched and pallid brows when thy keen
  lightnings blaze.

Una.

Make ready, Host Angelical ;—prepare !
From yonder planet, lo ! uplift your gaze ;
Be concentrated now the general Mind,
Absorbed the Soul collective now in prayer ;
The shrine descends of the Eternal God,
The heaven of heavens and sanctuary blest,
Wherein, Effulgence Absolute, he dwells ;
Revealed he comes in clouds of light and flame,
With whirlwinds of essential Spirits rapt,
Bright Cherubim, and love-lit Seraphim,
In his immediate effluence who rejoice,
Whirling for aye in mystic ecstasy,
And chaunting evermore the hymn of life ;
Wafted by those sweet harmonies through space,
By those celestial melodies upborne,
That shrine descends.   These congregated spheres,
A splendour inconceivable illumes,
They glow encompassed with the smile of God.

Lo, all ye Hosts uplift your mingled voice,
And greet united, the Eternal greet.

Hymn chaunted by the Heavenly Hosts.

Spirit Eternal and Essence of Light
Author of Being and Fountain of Might !
Trembling we rise all the Hosts of the spheres,
Thee to salute as thy glory appears,
Greeting the shrine of thy Presence descending,
Bright with the troops of thy seraphs attending.

Thrilled with that presence the tremulous air,
Breathing new vigour and joy everywhere,
Kindles our hearts in the glow of its rays,
Opens our lips into outbursts of praise ;
As a warm sun after tempest of shower,
Breaks a sweet globe into gardens of flower.

When thy great Love all pervading and free
Swells like the tide of an infinite sea,
We, as the shores that lie next to thy shrine,
Feel the first wave of its impulse divine ;
But in full flow ever onward it presses,
Everywhere touches and everywhere blesses.

Therefore to Thee in the wide Universe,
Who like ourselves may thy glory rehearse,
We that in suburbs of infinite light
Know all thy truth and thy love and thy might,
Far from the mists of the flesh and its blindness,
In the full glow of thy whole loving-kindness.

We who delight in the law of thy will,
Hail and adore Thee with rapturous thrill,
Now, as Thou comest to bless from above,
Moved by an impulse of infinite love ;
Sympathy quick in thanksgiving and praises,
Courses through all our angelical mazes.

Ministry blesséd and service of joy
On thy sweet missions our strength to employ,
Winging the truth through the worlds ; and the bliss
Then to rejoice in a triumph like this !
Darkness appalled by thy countenance glorious,
Furls her black flag at our progress victorious.

How thy effulgence of love and of light
Floods every sense with excess of delight :
Filled with thy Spirit electric each vein,
Burns with the glow of an exquisite pain,

Till overcome with exuberant splendour,
Falter our lips as thy praises we render.

As the Chorus ceases, God, veiled in his eternal sanctuary
and Holy of Holies, encompassed with countless spirits
chaunting divine harmonies, descends. The Heavens
are enveloped with an inconceivable blaze of light and
splendour.

Voice of God.

Hail to the Spirits of the blissful spheres,
Greeting unto ye all and salutation ;—
From those faint lights who tremble 'neath my gaze,
Young Cherubs newly born, to Powers sublime,
The golden clouds of deep-eyed Cherubim,
And lightning-laden blasts of Seraphim,
And terrible Archangels speeding swift
In worlds and stars to execute my will ;
In whom mine own eternal attributes
Incarnate I behold ; wisdom and love,
Grace, purity, enthronèd Majesty,
And beauty evanescent with swift gleam ;
In whom I live and act, aspire and know,
In whom love and create, suffer, enjoy,
Ruling through you the living Universe,

All worlds co-ordinating in their place,
And races guiding on their destined path,
The lesser by the loftier being swayed,
One spirit in ye all—one quickening flame,
Which from my central heart doth emanate ;
Ye lovely Angel choirs, in glittering swarms
And dazzling groups entangled intricate,
Ye glowing Constellations of bright souls,
My Stars effulgent and my blazing Suns,
Ye Dreams and Splendours of my hidden life,
Who throng beneath me in these gleaming plains,
And far and wide throb scintillant in space,
All Spirits, Angels, Powers, Divinities,
The salutation of the living God,
And benediction from on high receive.
All Hail !

The choruses combined of all the assembled Hosts.

In thy potent effulgence we kindle and burn, we glow
        in thy quickening rays ;
The sunshine of Love, we greet thee and hail the
        planets that whirl in thy blaze,
Thrilled with ecstasy keen we languish and faint, to
        thy glory renewing we turn,

O, glory of God—O rapture of Love—with thy in-
    finite passion we yearn.

Voice of God.

Well-pleased, I greet ye, Hosts Angelical,
And well pleased contemplate, with favouring eye,
Of this resplendent cosmic festival,
The high results ; ye who have hither sped,
Athwart the solemn voids at my command,
This noble race, my fragrant planet flower,
My stately tree, laden with luscious fruit
To consecrate, and guide upon the path
Of destiny.   Desist not from your task,
In yon light-beaming shrine, fair in my sight,
Full softly reared with labour that was prayer,
The chosen vessels of my love and grace
Communion hold ; high deeds are there ordained,
Great thoughts now hurtled forth by ardent minds,
Like stars that swim into the sea of night ;
There broods beneficent my Spirit pure,
With fostering wing, enkindling those pure souls
With joy and hope ; ye congregated Hosts,
Your full effulgence on that Temple shed,

Each mind therein with holy grace imbue,
And thrill with tidings of the love of God.

Choruses of all the Hosts.

We live in the light, we throb in the glow of Eternity's
    jubilant day,
With deity thrilled, in the infinite merged, we live
    thy will to obey.

Voice of God.

Serenely on this planet bright has dawned,
The blissful day of beatific calm,
But seldom in the lower globes beheld ;
These peoples blest their victory have won,
Transforming to a Paradise of Love,
Reflecting, mirror-like, the Heavenly spheres,
The kingdom temporal o'er which they reign.
In them asserted the supremacy
Ye now behold, in them made manifest,
Of mind o'er nature, soul o'er time and fate.
In freedom shall they walk henceforth and power,
Ruling in my great name their happy realm,
Fulfilling their appointed destiny,
Through endless time. With spreading sails, unfurled,

Obeying promptly the controlling hand,
Of skilful pilots by my will informed,
Well-set before the breeze, their gallant ship
E'en now majestic o'er these summer seas,
Has calmly swept.   The longed for hour has come,
The portals of the future opening wide ;
Day upward streameth golden in the East,
Their dedicated Seers fulfil their task,
New laws are promulgated and decrees,
The advent of the Era New they hail,
And now prepare, in majesty unveiled,
The satisfaction of the general hope,
To the assembled peoples to announce,
Attend, ye heavenly Hosts, glow, scintillate,
Pour forth on these enraptured Multitudes,
Of wisdom pure and love the effluent flame ;
Quicken and fructify in every mind,
The message and glad tidings of their Seers.

The luminous draperies that have enclosed the Temple
Beautiful are lifted as by a magic wand and float
cloud-like over the dome as when first witnessod.   The
convocation is again beheld by the assembled Multi-
tudes.

Queen of the Miranites.

Hearken, O ye happy peoples, to my voice attention
    pay,
On the wings of light it speedeth, lo ! it dawns, our
    blissful day ;
Fair the advent we have promised of propitious harmony
Smileth in serene fulfilment, born of love and melody,
From the glowing sky descendeth, radiant with celestial
    fire,
This the answer to our yearning, the response to our
    desire.
From this hour each home and homestead with new
    blessings shall be blest,
In each mind and heart henceforward heavenly grace
    made manifest,
Every soul with all partaking the enhanced collective
    weal,
Every heart with rapture welling, fountains pure which
    we unseal.
Lo, the atmosphere translucent, with new splendour
    how it glows,
With electrical vibrations how it trembles and o'er-
    flows,

As the morning's radiant chalice, with the sun's o'er-
brimming gold,

When the god ascends his chariot and begins his
journey bold,

Powers sublime are floating o'er us, dread divinities
aware,

Beatific they assemble, in the hushed expectant
air ;

With their presence our great purpose holy Spirits
dedicate,

Our desires and aspirations, they fulfil and consecrate,

They assist us ; they uphold us, and they hail our Era
New ;

Bright as their own heavenly mansions, pure as yon
celestial blue.

Swelling strains uplift ye peoples, ye who hear me,
mighty throng,

Celebrate our day of glory with heaven-soaring, sacred
song,

Voices sweet of all the nations fill the air with joy
and praise,

Greet with prayer and praise your Maker grateful on
this day of days.

Hymn of the Miranite people.

Now let us all upraise
To God our high defender,
　One voice of thanks and praise,
For all his love so tender;
　Who did from darkness lead
Our fathers in the past,
　And to their happy seed
Hath given peace at last.

　Stern Order's stately rule
'Twas their first task to fashion;
　Law in her iron school
Tamed each unruly passion;
　Till in restraint we saw
How lurked a common gain,
　How Freedom's fount was Law,
And Pleasure's parent Pain.

　Then fell this heavenly dream
Upon our holy sages,
　Which shed a hopeful beam
Upon our darker ages;

That jealousy should cease,
That each should fill his place,
That harmony and peace,
Should bind and bless the race.

What toils, what fears were theirs
Whose conquests we inherit,
Tis meet that we, their heirs,
Pay tribute to their merit :
And let us, as is fit,
In progress still ascend,
And age to age transmit,
New blessings without end.

So let us all upraise
To God our high defender,
One voice of thanks and praise,
For all his love so tender.
Who did from darkness lead,
Our fathers in the past,
And to their happy seed,
Brought harmony at last.

Voice of God.

My blessing on this planet I breathe forth,
And on this race my benediction breathe,
And on all races and Humanities,
That populate the living Universe,
And on the Heavenly Hosts.   My voice is heard,
And many-voiced the Universe replies :
Sweet voices, songs of praise, triumphal chaunts,
Ascending from the peoples blest below,
And from all living creatures in all worlds,
And from the angels of the heavenly spheres,
Commingling all in one full harmony,
The cosmic hymn, the Universal prayer,
Most welcome to my heart, acceptable,
Are rising to my throne.   Before me pass,
Those spheres, in multitudinous array,
A lovely vision of infinitude,
And visions of the souls who dwell thereon,
A beaming countenance innumerous,
With gratitude aglow, and love and joy,
Uplifted to my throne.   Enough.
Angelic Hosts your mission is achieved,
Return to your own realms, well satisfied,

There to pursue your countless destinies,
And in those varied kingdoms manifold
In all the orbs and glowing realms of space,
The planets and the congregated heavens,
In all your actions and in thought fulfil,
The will eternal of the Living God.

*Pause and inexpressible silence in all the heavens, in the
midst of which divine strains are heard, chaunted by
the spirits of the Sanctuary, dwelling in the immediate
effluence of Deity.*

Hymn chaunted by the Spirits of the Sanctuary.

In an ether of glory serene,
   In a shimmer of undulant light,
Where flashes of colour flit over the scene,
   Do we float in a sea of delight.

Where the spirit of God the Supreme
   With electrical effluence flows,
And our life in the light of a beautiful dream
   With perpetual happiness glows.

For a virtue steals into our thought,
   As we lie in the Spirit's embrace ;

And our souls into exquisite sympathy wrought,
   Every motive of Deity trace.

We behold the full scope of His will ;
   The fair works of His wisdom and love ;
And we feel as our senses with ecstasy thrill,
   Every impulse that flows from above.

Then our minds by His wisdom inspired,
   Are lit up with conceptions sublime,
And our hearts by the flame of His charity fired,
   Ever yearn toward the children of Time.

As we look far and wide from this height,
   With His eye of unlimited view,
We avail in the power of His infinite sight,
   To distinguish the false from the true.

Not alone the clear attributes bright
   That are bowed to by mortals below,
But apparent asperities seen in the light
   Of our vision with excellence glow :

Seeming opposites cease to contend ;
   For we see, while they wonder in awe,
How justice and mercy are balanced and blend,
   And how freedom is wedded to law.

In this ether of glory we seem,
   To dissolve in the breath of the shrine,
To pass out of ourselves as if into a dream
   And be lost in the spirit Divine.

*The Sanctuary of the Eternal Spirit, radiating flash-
ing splendours and stormful harmonies ascends and
disappears.*

Una.

Thus thinks and thus designs the Mind Eterne,
Thus feels and thus enjoys the cosmic Heart,
Thus palpitates the universal pulse,
Thus ebbs and flows the ever moving tide.
Spirit of God, for ever dost thou stream,
And interpenetrate nature and soul,
And thus for evermore, with answering throb,
From nature's realms, and from all living souls
Returneth to thy Source, rejubilant,

Of thy inflowing Presence the response,
Outflowing prayer and praise ; and this alone,
Throughout the ages of eternity,
This oscillation 'twixt the poles of being,
This rhythmical vibration tremulous
Is life ;—the pulse of God and beating heart.
Now Mira, that fair planet, blest indeed,
Thrice sanctified by the Eternal Love,
In happiness assured whirls on her course.
Our task is wrought.   Bright Hosts Angelical,
In prompt obedience to the Will Supreme,
To other worlds and other kingdoms flash
The lovely heavens that starred rejubilant
With light and joy and melody these plains,
Here gathered in magnificent array ;
Nor let us linger on our part.   Arise,
Glow forth resplendent Legions in your might,
Irradiate in fair majesty and strength ;
With will united let us breast the voids,
Athwart the wide infinitudes now seek,
Exulting seek, our own delightful realm,
There wafted by the breath of Thought and Love.

www.ingramcontent.com/pod-product-compliance
Lightning Source LLC
Chambersburg PA
CBHW030800020726
47499CB00006B/1711